# ONE HUMAN MINUTE

Publishers, as everyone knows, fear nothing so much as the publication of a book, since, according to Lem's Law, "No one reads; if someone does read, he doesn't understand; if he understands, he immediately forgets"—owing to general lack of time, the oversupply of books, and the perfection of advertising. The ad as the New Utopia is currently a cult phenomenon. We watch the dreadful or boring things on television, because (as public-opinion research has shown) after the sight of prattling politicians, bloody corpses strewn about various parts of the globe for various reasons, and dramatizations in which one cannot tell what is going on because they are never-ending serials (not only do we forget what we read, we also forget what we see), the commercials are a blessed relief.

# Stanislaw LEM

---

# ONE HUMAN MINUTE

*Translated by* CATHERINE S. LEACH

Mandarin

**A Mandarin Paperback**

ONE HUMAN MINUTE

First published in Great Britain 1986
by André Deutsch Limited
This edition published 1991
by Mandarin Paperbacks
Michelin House, 81 Fulham Road, London SW3 6RB

Mandarin is an imprint of the Octopus Publishing Group

English translation copyright © 1986 by
Harcourt Brace Jovanovich, Inc.

A CIP catalogue record for this title
is available from the British Library
ISBN 0 7493 0587 8

Printed and bound in Great Britain
by Cox & Wyman Limited, Reading, Berks

# CONTENTS

# ONE HUMAN MINUTE

# ONE HUMAN MINUTE

J. JOHNSON AND S. JOHNSON
MOON PUBLISHERS
*London—Mare Imbrium—New York, 1988*

## I

This book presents what all the people in the world are doing, at the same time, in the course of one minute. So says the Introduction. That no one thought of it sooner is surprising. It was simply begging to be written after *The First Three Minutes, The Cosmologist's Second,* and the *Guinness Book of World Records,* especially since they were best sellers (nothing excites publishers and authors today more than a book no one has to read but everyone needs to have). After those books, the idea was ready and waiting, lying in the street, needing only to be picked up. It would be interesting to know if "J. Johnson and S. Johnson" are man and wife, brothers, or just a pseudonym. I would like to see a photograph of these Johnsons. It is hard to explain why, but sometimes an author's appearance provides a key to a book. For me, at least, that has happened more than once. If a text is unconventional, reading it requires that one take a special approach. An author's face can then shed much light. My guess, though, is that the Johnsons do not exist, and that the "S." in front of the second Johnson is an allusion to

Samuel Johnson. But, then again, perhaps that is not important.

Publishers, as everyone knows, fear nothing so much as the publication of a book, since, according to Lem's Law, "No one reads; if someone does read, he doesn't understand; if he understands, he immediately forgets"—owing to general lack of time, the oversupply of books, and the perfection of advertising. The ad as the New Utopia is currently a cult phenomenon. We watch the dreadful or boring things on television, because (as public-opinion research has shown) after the sight of prattling politicians, bloody corpses strewn about various parts of the globe for various reasons, and dramatizations in which one cannot tell what is going on because they are never-ending serials (not only do we forget what we read, we also forget what we see), the commercials are a blessed relief. Only in them does paradise still exist. There are beautiful women, handsome men—all mature—and happy children, and the elderly have intelligence in their eyes and generally wear glasses. To be kept in constant delight they need only pudding in a new container, lemonade made from real water, a foot antiperspirant, violet-scented toilet paper, or a kitchen cabinet about which nothing is extraordinary but the price. The joy in the eyes of the stylish beauty as she beholds a roll of toilet paper or opens a cupboard like a treasure chest is transmitted instantly to everyone. In that empathy there also may be envy and even a little irritation, because everyone knows he could never experience ecstasy by drinking that lemonade or using that toilet paper. Everyone knows that this Arcadia is inaccessible, but its glow is effective nevertheless.

Anyway, it was clear to me from the start that advertising, as it improves in the merchandising struggle for existence, will enslave us not through the better quality of the goods it promotes but as a result of the ever-worsening quality of the world. After the death of God, of high ideals, of honor, of altruism, what is left to us in our overcrowded cities, under acid rains, but the ecstasy of these men and women of the ads as they announce crackers, puddings, and spreads like the coming of the Heavenly Kingdom? Because advertising, with monstrous effectiveness, attributes perfection to everything—and so to books, to every book—a person is beguiled by twenty thousand Miss Universes at once and, unable to decide, lingers unfulfilled in amorous readiness like a sheep in a stupor. So it is with everything. Cable television, broadcasting forty programs at once, produces in the viewer the feeling that, since there are so many, others must be better than the one he has on, so he jumps from program to program like a flea on a hot stove, proof that technological progress produces new heights of frustration. Although no one said it in so many words, we were promised the world, everything —if not to possess, at least to look at and touch. And literature (is it not but an echo of the world, its likeness and its commentary?) fell into the same trap. Why should I read about what particular individuals of different or the same sex say before going to bed, if there is no mention of the thousands of other, perhaps much more interesting people who do more imaginative things? There had to be a book, then, about what Everybody Else was doing, so that we would be tormented no longer by the doubt that we were reading nonsense while the Important Things were taking place Elsewhere.

The *Guinness Book* was a best seller because it presented nothing but exceptional things, with a guarantee of authenticity. This panopticon of records had, however, a serious drawback: it was soon obsolete. No sooner had some fellow eaten forty pounds of peaches complete with pits than another not only ate more, but died immediately after from a volvulus, which gave the new record a dismal piquancy. While it is untrue that there is no such thing as mental illness, that it was invented by psychiatrists to torment their patients and squeeze money out of them, it *is* true that normal people do far madder things than the insane. The difference is that the madman does what he does disinterestedly, whereas the normal person does it for fame, because fame can be converted into cash. Of course, some are satisfied with fame alone, so the matter is unclear. In any case, the still-surviving subspecies of intellectuals scorned this whole collection of records, and in polite society it was no distinction to remember how many miles someone on all fours could push a nutmeg with his nose painted lavender.

So a book had to be conceived that resembled the Guinness volume, was serious enough not to be dismissed with a shrug (like *The First Three Minutes*), but at the same time was not abstract, not loaded with theories about bosons and quarks. The writing of such a book—an honest, uncontrived book about everything at once, a book that would overshadow all others— seemed a total impossibility. Even I could not imagine the sort of book it would be. To the publishers I simply suggested writing a book that at worst would be the perfect antithesis of its advertising claims; but the idea did not take. Although the work I had in mind might have attracted readers, since the most important thing today is setting records, and the world's worst novel would have been a record, it was quite possible that even if I had succeeded, no one would have noticed.

How sorry I am not to have hit upon the better idea that gave birth to *One Human Minute*. Apparently, the publisher does not even have a branch on the Moon; "Moon Publishers," I am told, is only an advertising ploy. To avoid being called dishonest, the editor sent to the Moon, in a container on one of the Columbia shuttle flights, a copy of the manuscript and a small computer reader. If anyone challenged him, he could prove that part of the publishing operation actually did take place on the Moon, because the computer on the Mare Imbrium read the manuscript over and over. Perhaps it read without thinking, but that didn't matter: people in publishing houses on Earth generally read manuscripts the same way.

I should not have struck a satirical note at the beginning of my review, because there is nothing funny about this book.

You may feel indignation; you may take it as an affront to the entire human race, aimed so skillfully that it is irrefutable, containing nothing but verified facts; you may console yourself that at least no one can possibly make a film or a television series out of it—but it will definitely be worthwhile to think about it, though your conclusions will not be pleasant.

The book is unmistakably authentic and fantastic—if, like me, you take "fantastic" to mean that which goes beyond the limit of our conceptions. Not everyone will agree with me, but I remain convinced that the poverty of today's fantasy and science fiction lies in the fact that there is too little of the fantastic in it, in contrast to the reality that surrounds us. Thus, for example, it turns out that a person with his brain cut in two (there have been many such operations, especially on epileptics) both is and is not one individual. It happens that such a person, who appears completely normal, cannot put on trousers, because his right hand pulls them up while his left lowers them; or that he will embrace his wife with one arm while pushing her away with the other. It has been shown that in certain cases the right hemisphere of the brain does not know what the left sees and thinks; so it had to be acknowledged that the splitting of consciousness and even of personality had been achieved, that, in other words, two people existed in one body. But other experiments showed no such thing—not even that sometimes the individual would be single and sometimes double. The hypothesis that there were one and a half individuals, or two and something, also fell apart. This is no joke; the question of *how many* minds reside in such a person appears to have no answer, and this, indeed, is both real and fantastic. In this and only in this sense is *One Human Minute* fantastic.

Although each of us knows that on Earth all the seasons of the year, all climates, and all hours of the day and night exist together at every moment, we generally do not think about it. This commonplace, which every elementary-school student

knows, or should know, somehow lies outside our awareness—
perhaps because we do not know what to do with such an
awareness. Every night, electrons, forced to lick the screens of
our television sets with frenzied speed, show us the world
chopped up and crammed into the Latest News, so we can learn
what happened in China, in Scotland, in Italy, at the bottom of
the sea, on Antarctica, and we believe that in fifteen minutes we
have seen what has been going on in the whole world. Of course,
we have not. The news cameras pierce the terrestrial globe in
a few places: there, where an Important Politician descends the
steps of his plane and with false sincerity shakes the hands of
other Important Politicians; there, where a train has derailed—
but not just any derailment will do, only one with cars twisted
into spaghetti and people extracted piece by piece, because there
are already too many minor catastrophes. In a word, the mass
media skip everything that is not quintuplets, a coup d'état (best
if accompanied by a respectable massacre), a papal visit, or a
royal pregnancy. The gigantic, five-billion-human backdrop of
these events exists for certain, and anybody who was asked would
say, yes, of course he knows that millions of others exist; if he
thinks about it, he might even arrive at the fact that with every
breath he takes, so many children are born and so many people
die. It is, nevertheless, a vague knowledge, no less abstract than
the knowledge that, as I write this, an American probe stands
immobile in the pale sun on Mars, and that on the Moon lie the
wrecks of a couple of vehicles. The knowledge counts for nothing if it can be touched with a word but not experienced. One
can experience only a microscopic droplet out of the sea of
human destinies that surrounds us. In this respect a human
being is not unlike an amoeba swimming in a drop of water,
whose boundaries seem to be the boundaries of the world. The
main difference, I would say, is not our intellectual superiority
to the protozoon but the latter's immortality: instead of dying
it divides, thereby becoming its own, increasingly numerous
family.

So the task the authors of *One Human Minute* set themselves did not look plausible. In effect, were I to tell someone who has not yet seen the book that it contains few words, that it is filled with tables of statistics and columns of numbers, he would look upon the undertaking as a flop, even as insanity. Because what can be done with hundreds of pages of statistics? What images, emotions, and experiences can thousands of numbers evoke in our heads? If the book did not exist, if it were not lying on my desk, I would say the concept was original, even striking, but unrealizable, like the idea that reading the Paris and New York telephone books would tell you something about the inhabitants of those cities. If *One Human Minute* were not here in front of me, I would believe it to be as unreadable as a list of telephone numbers or an almanac.

Consequently, the idea—to show sixty seconds in the lives of all the human beings who coexist with me—had to be worked out as if it were a plan for a major campaign. The original concept, though important, was not enough to ensure success. The best strategist is not the one who knows he must take the enemy by surprise, but the one who knows how to do it.

What transpires on Earth even during a single second, there is no way of knowing. In the face of such phenomena, the microscopic capacity of human consciousness is revealed—our consciousness, that boundless spirit which we claim sets us apart from the animals, those intellectual paupers capable of perceiving only their immediate surroundings. How my dog frets each time he sees me packing my suitcase, and how sorry I am that I cannot explain to him that there is no need for his dejection, for the whimpers that accompany me to the front gate. There is no way to tell him that I'll be back tomorrow; with each parting he suffers the same martyrdom. But with us, it would seem, matters are quite different. We know what is, what can be; what we do not know, we can find out.

That is the consensus. Meanwhile, the modern world shows us at every step that consciousness is a very short blanket: it will

7

cover a tiny bit but no more, and the problems we keep having with the world are more painful than a dog's. Not possessing the gift of reflection, a dog does not know that he does not know, and does not understand that he understands nothing; we, on the other hand, are aware of both. If we behave otherwise, it is from stupidity, or else from self-deception, to preserve our peace of mind. You can have sympathy for one person, possibly for four, but eight hundred thousand is impossible. The numbers that we employ in such circumstances are cunning artificial limbs. They are like the cane a blind man uses; tapping the sidewalk keeps him from bumping into a wall, but no one will claim that with this cane he sees the whole richness of the world, or even the small fragment of it on his own street. So what are we to do with this poor, narrow consciousness of ours, to make it encompass what it cannot? What had to be done to present the one pan-human minute?

You will not learn everything *at once*, dear reader, but, glancing first at the table of contents and then at the respective headings, you will learn things that will take your breath away. A landscape composed not of mountains, rivers, and fields but of billions of human bodies will flash before you, as on a dark, stormy night a normal landscape is revealed when a flash of lightning rends the murk and you glimpse, for a fraction of a second, a vastness stretching toward all horizons. Though darkness sets in again, that image has now entered your memory, and you will not get rid of it. One can understand the visual part of this comparison, for who has not experienced a storm at night? But how can the world revealed by lightning be equated to a thousand statistical tables?

The device that the authors used is simple: the method of successive approximations. To demonstrate, let us take first, out of the two hundred chapters, the one devoted to death—or, rather, to dying.

Since humanity numbers nearly five billion, it stands to

reason that thousands die every minute. No revelation, that. Nevertheless, our narrow comprehension bumps into the figures here as if into a wall. This is easy to see, because the words "simultaneously nineteen thousand people die" carry not one iota more emotional weight than the knowledge that nine hundred thousand are dying. Be it a million, be it ten million, the reaction will always be the same: a slightly frightened and vaguely alarmed "Oh." We now find ourselves in a wilderness of abstract expressions; they mean something, but that meaning cannot be perceived, felt, experienced in the same way as the news of an uncle's heart attack. Learning of the Uncle's heart attack produces a greater impression on us.

But this chapter ushers you into dying for forty-eight pages. First come the data summaries, then the breakdown into specifics. In this way, you look first at the whole subject of death as through the weak lens of a microscope, then you examine sections in ever-increasing closeness as if using stronger and stronger lenses. First come natural deaths, in one category, then those caused by other people, in a separate category, then accidental deaths, acts of God, and so on. You learn how many people die per minute from police torture, and how many at the hands of those without government authorization; what the normal curve of tortures is over sixty seconds and their geographic distribution; what instruments are used in this unit of time, again with a breakdown into parts of the world and then by nation. You learn that when you take your dog for a walk, or while you are looking for your slippers, talking to your wife, falling asleep, or reading the paper, a thousand other people are howling and twisting in agony every consecutive minute of every twenty-four hours, day and night, every week, month, and year. You will not hear their cries but you will now know that it is continual, because the statistics prove it. You learn how many people die per minute by error, drinking poison instead of a harmless beverage. Again, the statistics take into account every

9

type of poisoning: weedkillers, acids, bases—and also how many deaths are the result of mistakes by drivers, doctors, mothers, nurses, and so on. How many newborns—a separate heading—are killed by their mothers just after birth, either on purpose or through carelessness: some infants are suffocated by a pillow; others fall into a privy hole, as when a mother, feeling pressure, thought it was a bowel movement, either through inexperience or mental retardation or because she was under the influence of drugs when the labor began; and each of these variants has further breakdowns. On the next page are newborns who die through no one's fault because they are monsters incapable of surviving, or because they are strangled by the umbilical cord, or because they fall victim to *placenta previa* or some other abnormality; again, I am not mentioning everything. Suicides take up a lot of space. Today there are far more ways of depriving oneself of life than in the past, and hanging has fallen to sixth place in the statistics. Moreover, the frequency-distribution table for new methods of suicide indicates that there has been an increase in methods since best-selling manuals have come out with instructions on making death swift and certain—unless someone wants to go slowly, which also happens. You can even learn, patient reader, what the correlation is between the size of the editions of these how-to suicide books and the normal curve of successful suicides. In the old days, when people were amateurs at it, more suicide attempts could be foiled.

Next, obviously, come deaths from cancer, from heart attacks, from the science of medicine, from the four hundred most important diseases; then come accidents, such as automobile collisions, death from falling trees, walls, bricks, from being run over by a train, from meteors even. Whether it is comforting to know that casualties from falling meteors are rare, I am not sure. As far as I can remember, 0.0000001 person per minute dies that way. Obviously, the Johnsons did solid work. In order to present the scope of death more accurately, they applied the so-called cross-reference, or diagonal method. Some tables will tell you from what group of causes people die; others, in what ways they die from a single cause—for example, electric shock. This method brings into relief the extraordinary wealth of our deaths. Death occurs most frequently from contact with an improperly grounded appliance, less often in the tub, and least often while urinating off a pedestrian bridge onto high-tension wires, this being only a fractional number per minute. In a footnote the conscientious Johnsons inform us that it is impossible to separate those who are killed deliberately by electric shock while under torture from those killed inadvertently when a little too much current is used.

There are also statistics on the means by which the living dispose of the dead, from funerals with cosmetic corpses, choirs, flowers, and religious pomp, to simpler and cheaper methods. We have many headings here, because, as it turns out, in the highly civilized countries more corpses are stuffed into bags with a stone—or cemented by their feet into old buckets, or cut up naked into pieces—and thrown into clay pits and lakes than in the Third World countries; more, too (another heading), are wrapped up in old newspapers or bloody rags and left in garbage dumps. The less well off are unacquainted with some of the ways of disposing of remains. Obviously, the information has yet to reach them, along with financial aid from the developed nations.

On the other hand, in poor countries more newborns are eaten by rats. These data appear on another page, but the reader will find a footnote directing him to the place, lest he miss them. And if he wants to take the book in small doses, he will find everything in the alphabetical index.

One cannot maintain for long that these are dry, boring figures that say nothing. One begins to wonder morbidly how many other ways people are dying every minute one reads, and the fingers turning the pages become moist. It is sweat, of course; it can hardly be blood.

Death by starvation (there had to be a separate table for it, with a breakdown by age; most who starve to death are children) carries a footnote telling us that it is only valid for the year of publication, since the numbers increase rapidly and in arithmetical progression. Death from overeating happens, too, of course, but is 119,000 times rarer. These data contain an element of exhibitionism and an element of blackmail.

I intended only to glance at this chapter, but then read as if compelled, like someone who peels the bandage off his bleeding wound to look, or who probes the cavity in his aching tooth with a toothpick: it hurts, but it is hard to stop. The figures are like a tasteless, odorless drug that seeps into the brain. And yet I have not mentioned—and have no intention of listing—the data on marasmus, senility, lameness, degeneration of organs, for then I would be quoting the book, whereas my task is only to review it.

Actually, the columns of figures arranged in tabular form for all types of deaths—those bodies of children, old people, women, and newborns of all nations and races, bodies present in spirit behind the numbers—are not the most sensational part of the book. Having written that sentence, I ask myself if I am being honest, and I repeat: no, they are not the most sensational. The enormity of all this human dying is a little like one's own death: it is anticipated, but only generally and vaguely, the way we comprehend the inevitability of our own end, though we do not know the form that it will take.

The real immensity of flesh-and-blood life manifests itself on the very first page. The facts are indisputable. One might indeed entertain doubts about the accuracy of the data in the chapter on dying: they are based on averages, after all, and it is hard to believe that the taxonomy and etiology of the deaths were rendered with complete exactitude. But the honest authors do not conceal from us the possible statistical deviations. Their Introduction thoroughly describes the methods of calculation and even includes references to the computer programs employed. Though the methods allow for standard deviations, the latter have no importance for the reader—what difference does it really make if 7,800 newborns die per minute or 8,100? Besides, these deviations are insignificant because they tend to cancel one another out. The number of births is indeed not uniform for all times of the year and day; but since on Earth all times of the day, night, and year simultaneously coexist, the sum of stillbirths remains constant. Some columns, however, contain data arrived at by indirect inference. For example, neither the police nor private murderers—whether professional or amateur (not counting the ideological variety)—publish statistics on the effectiveness of their work. The error in magnitude here can be considerable.

On the other hand, the statistics of Chapter One are beyond reproach. They tell how many people there are—and thus how many living human bodies—in each minute of the 525,600 minutes of the year. How many bodies means: the amount of muscle, bone, bile, blood, saliva, cerebrospinal fluid, excrement, and so on. Naturally, when the thing to be visualized is of a very great order of magnitude, a popularizer readily resorts to comparative imagery. The Johnsons do the same. So, were all humanity taken and crowded together in one place, it would occupy three hundred billion liters, or a little less than a third of a cubic kilometer. It sounds like a lot. Yet the world's oceans hold 1,285 million cubic kilometers of water, so if all humanity —those five billion bodies—were cast into the ocean, the water level would rise less than a hundredth of a millimeter. A single splash, and Earth would be forever unpopulated.

Games of this sort with statistics can rightly be called cheap. They may be meant as a reminder that we—who with the might of our industry poisoned the air, the soil, the seas, who turned jungles into deserts, who exterminated countless species of animals and plants that had lived for hundreds of millions of years, who reached other planets, and who altered even the albedo of the Earth, thereby revealing our presence to cosmic observers—could disappear so easily and without a trace. However, I was not impressed. Nor was I impressed by the calculation that 24.9 billion liters of blood could be poured from all mankind and it would not make a Red Sea, not even a lake.

After this, under an epigraph from T. S. Eliot saying that existence is "birth, and copulation, and death," come new figures. Every minute, 34.2 million men and women copulate. Only 5.7 percent of all intercourse results in fertilization, but the combined ejaculate, at a volume of forty-five thousand liters a minute, contains 1,990 billion (with deviations in the last decimal place) living spermatozoa. The same number of female eggs could be fertilized sixty times an hour with a minimal ratio of one spermatozoon to one egg, in which impossible case three million children would be conceived per second. But this, too, is only a statistical manipulation.

Pornography and our modern life style have accustomed us to the forms of sexual life. You would think that there was nothing left to reveal, nothing to show that would shock. But, presented in statistics, it comes as a surprise. Never mind the game of comparisons which is put to use again: for instance, the stream of sperm, forty-three tons of it, discharged into vaginas per minute—its 430,000 hectoliters is compared with the 37,-850 hectoliters of boiling water produced at each eruption of the largest geyser in the world (at Yellowstone). The geyser of sperm is 11.3 times more abundant and shoots without intermission. The image is not obscene. A person can be aroused sexually only within a certain range of magnitudes. Acts of copulation, when shown in great reduction or great enlargement, do not elicit any sexual response. Arousal, an inborn reaction, occurs as a reflex in certain centers in the brain, and does not manifest itself in conditions that exceed visual norms. Sexual acts seen in reduced dimensions leave us cold, for they show creatures the size of ants.

Magnification, on the other hand, arouses disgust, because the smoothest skin of the most beautiful woman will then look like a porous, pale surface from which protrude hairs as thick as fangs, while a sticky, glistening grease oozes from the ducts of the sebaceous glands.

The surprise I spoke of has a different cause. Humanity pumps 53.4 billion liters of blood per minute, but that red river is not surprising; it must flow to sustain life. At the same time, humanity's male organs eject forty-three tons of semen, and the point is that though each ejaculation is also an ordinary physiological act, for the individual it is irregular, intimate, not overly frequent, and even not necessary. Besides, there are millions of old people, children, voluntary and involuntary celibates, sick people, and so forth. And yet that white stream flows with the same constancy as the red river system. The irregularity disappears when the statistics take in the whole Earth, and that is what surprises. People sit down to tables set for dinner, look for refuse in garbage dumps, pray in chapels, mosques, and churches, fly in planes, ride in cars, sit in submarines carrying nuclear missiles, debate in parliaments; billions sleep, funeral processions walk through cemeteries, bombs explode, doctors bend over operating tables, thousands of college professors simultaneously enter their classrooms, theater curtains lift and drop, floods swallow fields and houses, wars are waged, bulldozers on battlefields push uniformed corpses into ditches; it thunders and lightnings, it is night, day, dawn, twilight; but no matter what happens that forty-three-ton impregnating stream of sperm flows without stop, and the law of large numbers guarantees that it will be as constant as the sum of solar energy striking Earth. There is something mechanical about this, inexorable, and animallike. How can one come to terms with an image of humanity copulating relentlessly through all the cataclysms that befall it, or that it has brought upon itself?

Well, there you have it. Keep in mind that it is impossible

to summarize a book that reduces human affairs to a minimum
—that is, to numbers (there is no more radical method of cramming phenomena together). The book itself is an extract, an
extreme abbreviation of humanity. In a review one cannot even
touch on the most remarkable chapters. Mental illnesses: it turns
out that today there are more lunatics in any given minute than
all the people who lived on Earth for the last several dozen
generations. It is as if all of previous humanity consisted, today,
of madmen. Tumors—in my first medical work thirty-five years
ago I called them a "somatic insanity," in that they are a suicidal
turning of the body upon itself—are an exception to life's rule,
an error in its dynamics, but that exception, expressed in the
statistics, is an enormous Moloch. The mass of cancerous tissue,
calculated per minute, is a testimony to the blindness of the
processes that called us into existence. A few pages farther on
are matters even more dreary. I pass over in silence the chapters
on acts of violence, rape, sexual perversion, bizarre cults and
organizations. The picture of what people do to people, to humiliate them, degrade them, exploit them, whether in sickness,
in health, in old age, in childhood, in disability—and this incessantly, every minute—can stun even a confirmed misanthrope
who thought he had heard of every human baseness. But enough
of this.

Was this book necessary? A member of the French Academy, writing in *Le Monde*, said that it was inevitable, it had to
appear. This civilization of ours, he wrote, which measures everything, counts everything, evaluates everything, weighs everything, which breaks every commandment and prohibition,
desires to know all. But the more populous it becomes, the less
intelligible it is to itself. It throws itself with the most fury at
whatever continues to resist it. There was nothing strange,
therefore, in its wanting to have its own portrait, a faithful
portrait, such as never existed, and an objective one—objectivity
being the order of the day. So in the cause of modern technology

it took a photograph like those done with a reporter's flash camera: without touch-ups.

The old gentleman dodged the question about the need for *One Human Minute*, saying that it appeared because, as the product of its time, it had to appear. The question, however, remains. I would substitute for it another, more modest question: Does this book truly show all of humanity? The statistical tables are a keyhole, and the reader, a Peeping Tom, spies on the huge naked body of humanity busy about its everyday affairs. But through a keyhole not everything can be seen at once. More important, perhaps, is the fact that the observer stands eye to eye, as it were, not merely with his own species but with its fate. One has to admit that *One Human Minute* contains a great deal of impressive anthropological data in the chapters on culture, beliefs, rituals, and customs, because, although these are numerical agglomerations (or maybe for precisely that reason), they demonstrate the astonishing diversity of people who are, after all, identical in their anatomy and physiology. It is curious that the number of languages people employ cannot be calculated. No one knows precisely how many there are; all we know is that there are over four thousand. Even the specialists have not identified all of them. The fact that some small ethnic groups take their languages with them when they die out makes the matter even more difficult to settle. On top of that, linguists are not in agreement about the status of certain languages, considered by some to be dialects, by others separate taxonomic entities. Few are the cases, however, where the Johnsons admit defeat in the conversion of all data to events per minute. Yet it is just in such cases that one feels—at least I felt—a kind of relief. This is a matter with philosophical roots.

In an elite German literary periodical I came across a review of *One Human Minute* written by an angry humanist. The book makes a monster out of mankind, he said, because it has built a mountain of meat from bodies, blood, and sweat (the measurements include, beyond excrement and menstrual bleeding, various kinds of sweat, since sweat from fear is different from sweat from hard work), but it has amputated the heads. One cannot equate the life of the mind with the number of books and newspapers that people read, or of the words they utter per minute (an astronomical number). Comparing theater-attendance and television-audience figures with the constants of death, ejaculation, etc., is not just misleading but a gross error. Neither orgasm nor death is exclusively and specifically human. What is more, they are largely physiological in character.

On the other hand, data that *are* specifically human, such as matters of intellect, are not exhausted, but neither are they explained by the size of the editions of philosophical journals or works. It is as if someone were to try to measure the heat of passion with a thermometer, or to put, under the heading "Acts," both sex acts and acts of faith. This categorical chaos is no accident, for the authors' intention was precisely to shock the reader with a satire made of statistics—to degrade us all under a hail of figures. To be a person means, first of all, to have a life of the spirit, and not an anatomy subject to addition, division, and multiplication. The very fact that the life of the spirit cannot be measured and put in statistical form refutes the authors' claim to have produced a portrait of humanity. In this bookkeeper's breakdown of billions of people into functional pieces to fit under headings, one sees the efficiency of a pathologist dissecting a corpse. Perhaps there is even malice. Indeed, among the thousands of index entries there is nothing at all resembling "human dignity."

Another critic also struck at the philosophical roots I mentioned. I have the impression (I say this parenthetically) that *One Human Minute* threw the intellectuals into confusion. They felt that they had the right to ignore such products of mass culture as the *Guinness Book,* but *One Human Minute* confounded them. For the Johnsons—whether they are cautious or only cunning—raised their work to a much higher level with a methodical, scholarly introduction. They anticipated many objections, citing contemporary thinkers who call truth the prime value in society. If that is so, then all truth, even the most depressing, is permissible and even necessary.

The critic-philosopher put his foot in the stirrup held by the Johnsons and mounted that high horse. First he praised them, then found fault with them. We have been treated—he wrote in *Encounter*—almost literally the way Dostoevsky feared in his *Notes from Underground*. Dostoevsky believed that we were threatened by scientifically proven determinism, which would toss the sovereignty of the individual—with its free will —onto the garbage heap when science became capable of predicting every decision and every emotion like the movements of a mechanical switch. He saw no alternative, no escape from the cruel predictability that would deprive us of our freedom, except madness. His Underground Man was prepared to lose his mind, so that, released by madness, it would not succumb to triumphant determinism.

But now that flimsy determinism of the nineteenth-century rationalists has collapsed and will rise no more; it was replaced, with unexpected success, by probability theory and statistics. The fates of individuals are as unpredictable as the paths of individual particles of gas, but from the great number of both emerge laws that pertain to all together, though the laws are not concerned with individual molecules or persons. After the fall of determinism, therefore, science executed a circling maneuver and attacked the Underground Man from another side.

Unfortunately, it is untrue that there is no hint of humanity's spiritual life in *One Human Minute*. Locking up that life inside the head, so that it will manifest itself only in words, is an understandable habit of professional literati and other intellectuals, who constitute (the book informs us) a microscopic particle, a millionth, of humanity. The life of the spirit is displayed, by 99 percent of people, through actions that are measurable to the highest degree, and it would be a mistake to assume high-mindedly that psychopaths, murderers, and pimps have any less psyche than water carriers, merchants, and weavers.

So one cannot accuse the authors of misanthropy; at the most, one can point to the limitations inherent in their method. The originality of *One Human Minute* lies in its being not a statistical compilation of information about what has taken place, like an ordinary almanac, but rather *synchronous* with the human world, like a computer of the type that we say works in real time, a device tracking phenomena as they occur.

Having thus crowned the authors, the critic from *Encounter* proceeded to trim the laurels he had bestowed as he took up the Introduction. The demand for truth, which the Johnsons wave like a banner in order to defend *One Human Minute* against charges of obscenity, sounds fine but is unworkable in practice. The book does not contain "everything about the human being," because that is impossible. The largest libraries in the world do not contain "everything." The quantity of anthropological data discovered by scientists now exceeds any individual's ability to assimilate it. The division of labor, including intellectual labor, begun thirty thousand years ago in the Paleolithic, has become an irreversible phenomenon, and there is nothing that can be done about it. Like it or not, we have placed our destiny in the hands of the experts. A politician is, after all, a kind of expert, if self-styled. Even the fact that competent experts must serve under politicians of mediocre intelligence and little foresight is a problem that we are stuck with, because the experts themselves cannot agree on any major world issue. A logocracy of quarreling experts might be no better than the rule of the mediocrities to which we are subject. The declining intellectual quality of political leadership is the result of the growing complexity of the world. Since no one, be he endowed with the highest wisdom, can grasp it in its entirety, it is those who are least bothered by this who strive for power. It is no accident that in the chapter on mental ability in *One Human Minute* there is no I.Q. information for eminent statesmen. Even the ubiquitous Johnsons were not able to subject those people to intelligence tests.

My view of this book is undramatic. One can approach it in a thousand ways, as this article shows. In my opinion, the book is neither a malicious satire nor the honest truth; not a caricature and not a mirror. The asymmetry of *One Human Minute*, its inclusion of incomparably more shameful human evil than manifestations of good, and more of the misery of our existence than its beauty, I attribute neither to the authors' intention nor to their method. Only those who still cherish illusions on the subject of Man can be depressed by the book. The asymmetry of good and evil would probably even lend itself to a numerical comparison, though the Johnsons somehow did not think of it. The chapters on vice, felony, fraud, theft, blackmail, and computer crime* are far more extensive than the chapters devoted to "good deeds." The authors did not compare such numbers in one table, and that is a pity. It would have shown clearly how much more extensive evil is than good. Fewer are the ways of helping people than of harming them; it is the nature of things, not a consequence of the statistical method. Our world does not stand halfway between heaven and hell; it seems much closer to hell. Free of illusions in this respect—for some time now—I was not shocked by this book.

---

*This involves the manipulation of this electronic extension of intellectual work to bring unlawful profits to the programmer. Recently it has expanded to include activities that, at the moment, are not recognized as crimes, on the principle of *nullum crimen sine lege*: it is not criminal to use the huge processing power of computers to increase one's chances of winning the lottery or in gambling. A couple of mathematicians showed that you could break the bank in roulette by analyzing the movements of the ball, for no roulette wheel is completely random; that is, the wheel deviates from theoretical chance, and the deviation can be determined and exploited by computer.

## II

The second edition of *One Human Minute* has been expanded by its publisher to include several new chapters; therefore, a fresh discussion is in order.

This time, the book opens with a picture of the world as mankind's habitation. Such data can be found in any encyclopedia, but when they are converted to per-minute quantities, they undeniably produce a greater impression than do the dry, abstract entries in a reference book. It is indeed curious to realize that there is always a storm raging somewhere on Earth, and that the number of lightning bolts is constant: six thousand per minute. One hundred strike every second, and that means perpetually, month after month and century after century. We also learn here that the Earth covers 1,800 kilometers in the course of a minute of orbiting the Sun. In the same short interval of time, the combined weight of the cosmic "debris" falling constantly on the Earth's surface amounts to thousands of tons. At the same time, our planet loses a considerable amount of its atmosphere, which, stirred by the movements of barometric high and lows, by cyclones and tradewinds, and also heated by the sun, creates its own "tail" stretching for many thousands of miles; the Earth loses, as a result, an enormous quantity of gas. New gases, however, constantly escape from the Earth's depths; the oceans also emit them, partly as water vapor; and so on. The book, then, commences in the style of popular science. The figures reveal at once the vastness of the planet in relation to its inhabitants and the incredible minuteness of the planet in relation to the universe. But it is all, as I said, a laborious extract of natural-history textbooks.

Some of the chapters previously described have been enlarged by the authors with data now of a humorous, now of a macabre cast. Man as executioner, oppressor, and killer of his own species was presented to us in the first edition. Now we see what a predator he is, or, if you will, what a parasite of the entire biosphere—that is, the animal and plant kingdoms. Almost nobody sitting down to a steak or chop feels any pang of conscience; we do not even think that in our complicity with the butchers we are like one who aids a killer in the disposal of the victim's remains. In order that the thought should never come to mind and interfere with our consumption of tasty morsels, all languages—without exception—have created a separate vocabulary which gives us special consideration. We *pass away;* animals can only *die.* And, of course, every dictionary of hunting jargon unfailingly exonerates all that is synonymous, in every legal language, with premeditated murder, since a hunter goes into the woods with a loaded weapon for the express purpose of killing. *One Human Minute* goes to the heart of the matter, cutting through these pharisaical subtleties of our vocabulary, for it gives not the names but the numbers of the victims. Every minute, it turns out, mountains of animal corpses fall at our hands, and the same mountains of corpses, in the form of roasts, are chewed by several billion human teeth per minute. These are like images from Gulliver's travels to Brobdingnag, where a lady giant's enticing smile might be a scene out of *Jaws,* with the shark opening its monstrous mouth. As we know, the brain of a live monkey eaten raw from the opened skull with a spoon is a sophisticated Chinese delicacy; and though it is unlikely that the quantity of brains consumed per minute in this way could have been established with much accuracy, one does find the figure under the heading "Exotic Dishes."

To the eternally shooting geyser of semen this edition has added the river of milk that flows from the breasts of women all over the world into the mouths of infants.

The human disfigurations that are set apart in a separate chapter—no doubt for more powerful effect—are a silent, natural expression of our fate. It is as if whoever set up this table— these armies of the blind and deaf, these millions of bodies deformed from birth and by their very number proving how little Nature truly cares about the individual human being (yet in all religions and nearly all philosophical systems we try so hard to preserve the human dignity of the individual), and these separately (pedantically) enumerated infirmities of old age—it is as if the author of this table wanted to compare the aged with rusting wrecks or derelict machines, which, though slowly disintegrating, preserve for a while their original contours.

Even medical procedures intended to maintain and save life are shown in their consequences in the chapter on disfigurations. There are mobs of armless and legless people after amputations; and radical surgery, the prevailing method of fighting cancer, now bestows upon the world, every minute, so many women with mastectomies, so many of both sexes sterilized, or with portions of intestines and stomachs removed. It is hard to run one's eyes all the way down these columns of figures.

I am not alone in suspecting that the editors wished to intensify the "impact" of a book that, after all, like any thick volume of statistics, hardly makes for easy reading. The new chapters serve just this purpose, especially the highlighting of the figures dealing with children. Before, this subject was scattered under different headings, but now it has been decided to pull it together for easier viewing. The effect is nightmarish. The question again arises whether such information should be set forth in so cold and dry a manner, since the reader can react only with impotent grief, horror, and depression.

For a number of years now in the illustrated magazines of the wealthy nations there have appeared, fairly frequently, large ads showing photographs of a small child, usually swarthy and dark-haired; the charitable organization sponsoring the ad requests donations to save such children from starvation. And, again, we learn from the brutally accurate statistics that the number of children saved in this manner, compared with the number left to their fate, is a drop in the ocean. One might say that great moral wisdom lies in the statement from the old Mosaic law: "He who saves the life of one human being saves the world." Perhaps, but that sort of commentary is absent from *One Human Minute*.

Since statistics give averages—often amusing us with facts like "Every husband is unfaithful 2.67 times a year"—and one of the qualities that distinguish our species from all others is the enormous range of life styles (luxury and poverty, for example, both equally unmerited), the book uses the so-called diagonal method along with print of different colors to dramatize just this range of fortunes. The commentary distinguishes the text from the *Guinness Book:* the latter focuses on the oddities of human behavior, on senseless stunts, whereas here the object is to *contrast* the affluent consumer societies, with their constantly increasing wealth, with those societies headed toward disaster. There are many comparisons—the energy used per minute per person in wealthy as opposed to poor countries, for example, which gives a clear picture of the ruinous poverty where dried dung or wood serves as fuel. *One Human Minute* goes beyond the boundary of its title here, providing other figures: for example, the forests in poor countries, cut down much faster than Nature can replace them, will revert to wasteland.

The financial side of things has also been given more space. It is not a trivial matter to learn the price tag of humanity's religious beliefs (again, compared—maliciously—with the cost of arms). The treatment of church collections, tithes, and contributions as *capital investments* per minute, interest on which is to be paid out in the hereafter, speaks for itself. The commentary on these statistics disclaims any intention of scoffing, the issue being only the cost of maintaining religious institutions, a cost that is measurable whether or not "otherworldly dividends" are paid. (Added to the cost: the upkeep and overhead of cloistered orders, missions, and training for clergy of all faiths.) In a word, we learn how much humanity spends to "maintain good relations with the Lord."

The sections on sexuality have also been revised and enlarged. An introductory comment explains what changes have occurred since the first edition of *One Human Minute*. In those few years the sex industry grew exponentially; most of the previous edition's figures were therefore out of date. A veritable panopticon opens up before us here, with astonishing descriptions and numbers. Descriptions are needed, because for anyone unacquainted with the products in this branch of consumer industry, the terms alone will be completely unintelligible. As a satirist of the women's movement remarked not very long ago, women were discriminated against in the matter of "bionic dolls," because there were various artificial females—complete with built-in tape recorders, so that with various cassettes they could express themselves charmingly or obscenely, according to taste—but almost no male dolls for sale. The situation has improved to a point where equality of the sexes has nearly been achieved. The dolls, battery-powered and self-charging, and therefore portable, work so well that they can actually pair up and dispense with living partners altogether. Ridiculous. But the hunger for sexual experience does seem to be insatiable in affluent nations of the "permissive" type. It turns out that they spend more on lingerie, gowns, cosmetics, wigs, and perfumes for these artificial partners—per minute—than the countries of the Third World spend on all their clothing essentials.

Data that could not be established or even statistically approximated, such as how many women are raped per minute, are presented, with scrupulous qualifications, as conjectures: the experts of this sad phenomenon maintain that the majority of rape victims hide their shame in silence. Since, however, no one of either sex today need be ashamed of homosexuality or conceal it, *One Human Minute* presents their several-million-strong ranks with great numerical precision.

As we leaf through this thick volume—thicker than the first edition—we encounter, from time to time, data that tell us that we live in an era where the flowering of art is barely distinguishable from its demise. The rules and boundaries that distinguish art from what cannot be art have eroded completely and disappeared. Thus, on the one hand, more works of art are being created in the world than cars, planes, tractors, locomotives, and ships combined. On the other hand, that great volume is lost, as it were, in the still greater volume of objects that have no use whatever. For me these numbers gave rise to black thoughts. First, the world of art has been shattered once and for all, and no art lover can piece things together again, even if he is only interested in one area, like painting or sculpture. One might think that the technology of communication had advanced for the express purpose of revealing to us the microscopic capacity of the human brain. What good is it if everything that is beautiful lies at our disposal, and can even be called up on the screen of a home computer, if we are—again—like a child facing the ocean with a spoon? And, as I glanced at the tables of how many different kinds of "works of art" are made per minute (and of what materials), I was saddened by the banality of those works. If archaeologists in the distant future make excavations to learn what kind of graphic art was produced in our era, they will find nothing. They will not be able to distinguish our everyday garbage and litter from our "works of art," because often there is no objective difference between them. That a can of Campbell's tomato soup is a work of art is the result of its being put on exhibit, but when it lies in some dump no one will ever gaze upon it in aesthetic rapture like an archaeologist contemplating the vase or marble goddess he has recovered from the Greek silt. One might conclude that the real intention of the authors of *One Human Minute* was not to give us a frozen moment of the human world, a cross section cut with a gigantic knife, but instead to bury us beneath an avalanche of numbers proving how close we have come to the anecdote about the flies (a pair of flies, after one season of unchecked proliferation, will cover the oceans and the earth with a layer of insects half a mile deep).

Again we have the dilemma on which the first critics of this book broke their teeth. Is the terrible predominance of evil over good, of malice over loving kindness, of stupidity over intelligence, the true balance sheet of the human world? Or is it the result, in part, of the computers and the statistical viewpoint?

It is easier to give the tonnage per minute that the sex industry produces—the mountains of genital appliances, photographs, special clothing, chains, whips, and other accessories that facilitate the application of our reproductive physiology to perverted practices—than to measure, weigh, or simply *observe* human love in its nontechnological manifestations. Surely, when people love one another—and it is hard to doubt that there are hundreds of millions who do—when they remain faithful to their erotic or parental feelings, there is no measure, no apparatus, that can record *that* and grind it in the statistical mill. With sadomasochism, on the other hand, with rape, murder, or any perversion, there are no such difficulties: statistical theory is at our service.

The industrialization of emotion in all its aspects—say the indignant critics of *One Human Minute*—is an utter impossibility. There cannot be, nor ever will be, devices, harnesses, salves, aphrodisiacs, or any sort of "meters" to abet or measure filial or maternal love; no thermometers to gauge the heat of lovers' passions. That their temperature is sometimes fatally high, we learn only indirectly from the statistics on suicides resulting from unrequited love. Such love is out of fashion in the modern world, and any writer who devotes his works to love alone will not make it into the literary Parnassus.

There is no denying the merit of such arguments as these; the trouble is that without the backing of facts and figures they remain generalities. The publishers of *One Human Minute* failed not only to establish the I.Q. of politicians; they were also unable to include a register of the sins confessed per minute in the Catholic confessional, or of those acts of kindness whose authors wished to remain anonymous. And so the argument over the precise degree of objectivity or subjectivity of this book cannot be settled.

With the help of the alphabetical index, anyone who seeks an answer to a particular question can easily locate the relevant data. It is true that the conclusions drawn from data combined in this way are far from unequivocal. Even today, five billion human brains process less information per minute than do computers in the same time; computers make possible the solution of problems and the execution of tasks otherwise beyond reach.

Automated telephone communication on a global scale is a splendid thing, no question. But it did produce a by-product —numerically not insignificant—that is, telephone sex. In the last few years, agencies offering such services have mushroomed. You have but to pick up the receiver, dial, and give your credit-card number in order to avail yourself of your favorite variety of conversational lewdness—copulating in words, so to speak— with an Australian, say, while you sit in Ontario. But, then, no one can deny that the split between technological progress and moral progress has taken place and is irreversible—impossible though it may be to establish the date of this separation, which marks the collapse of our nineteenth-century faith in the collective march into the happy future. Technological solutions to one's desires can serve evil as well as good. But goodness, again, is not measurable, and sometimes it happens that neither concept can be pinned down. In *One Human Minute,* for example, we learn how many scientific works are published every minute, and also how very little of his own field a scientist can assimilate, even superficially. There is more and more information that he *ought* to be aware of but that exceeds his physiological capacity of absorption. Today only supercomputers know everything in every field.

Looking under the proper heading, one learns what computers—which seem to be changing from assistants to managers of our civilization—can accomplish in one minute. Models of the newest generation can perform nearly a billion logical operations in that interval. But a fragmentary look will not tell us what is really going on in science. Perhaps for that reason—or to give the book greater weight, without diminishing its readability—an extensive afterword was included, in addition to the commentaries introducing each chapter to the reader. This is actually an essay presenting the methods of calculation employed in *One Human Minute.* In more than one case they smack of detective work, almost in the spirit of Sherlock Holmes. But the infallibility of Holmes's famous deductions, which he was able to make from an old hat, a forgotten pipe, a cane, or a watch, re-creating from them the unknown owner's appearance, station in life, and character traits—for example, that the person had recently fallen on hard times—all that brilliant detection was due to the assistance given to Holmes secretly by the author. But countless parodies have since ridiculed that "classic deduction," showing how from the same clues one might construct many logically tight but mutually exclusive hypotheses. No brilliant detective-statistician was in a position, however, to bring forth this book singlehandedly, nor could a large team of mathematicians have done it; computers were needed. A great deal of the work was done mechanically, that is, by converting known and accessible data to the unit of time indicated in the title. When data were unavailable, they had to be arrived at in a roundabout way, by searching for correlations (there is a high positive correlation, for example, between an accident at a power station that cuts current to a big city or area of a country and the number of children born roughly nine months later). Where we are dealing with single phenomena (and it was precisely with these that Sherlock Holmes grappled), the well-chewed mouthpiece of a pipe might testify to the smoker's strong jaws and his attachment to that pipe and no other, though he has a large collection, or it might simply be the result of a nervous tic, or, finally, the pipe might not be his property at all—he might have found it, stuck it into his pocket, then got himself murdered, in which case the pipe would be a red herring.

Five billion people, on the other hand, is a big enough aggregate to be governed by the laws of large numbers. Nothing is simpler than predicting the number of automobile accidents under specific weather conditions and a given volume of traffic. But how do we arrive at the number of accidents (say, per minute) that did not take place but were "close calls"? Or, as someone said more pointedly, how do we calculate the danger of driving, given the fact that heavy metropolitan traffic represents the sum of miraculously averted crashes? We can, it turns out, although only the accidents that actually take place leave behind evidence in the form of dented cars and sometimes corpses. Between the "unrealized collisions" and the collisions that do occur, with the number of dead and injured, with the frequency according to road surface and quantity of vehicles, there exist definite mathematical ratios, and one can make use of them. This is still a relatively simple matter.

Some calculations were merely tedious and complicated, but did not require any special ingenuity on the part of the programmers. There was the amusing idea of comparing the global circulation of money with the circulation of red corpuscles, except that money does not pass from vessel to vessel but from hand to hand, and does not even physically participate in the transaction, because it consists of electronic impulses that change the balances in bank accounts. Despite bank confidentiality, a team of *One Human Minute* researchers secured the global payments-per-minute figures. By way of illustration, a small map of the Earth was put above the statistics, the "flow of currency" resembling the lines on a meteorological map. It is evident that considerable effort was put into imagery in this new edition, for often such data do not easily lend themselves to visualization. One could say that *One Human Minute* became a reality thanks to the collaboration of the publisher's computers and the computers of nearly the entire world, and humanity was the raw material they processed.

Formerly, when a central data bank of drivers with traffic violations did not exist, one could not obtain the necessary information with such wonderful precision. The number of people who travel by plane per minute can easily be established from the statistics on the utilization of passenger seats for all the airlines, information that is readily available. Corporate secrecy and the confidentiality of the medical (or legal) profession presented obstacles. There was also the problem of the "guesstimate" or "dark number": of incidents that happened, for example, but were not made public (as in the case of rape). Yet these numbers are not pulled out of a hat; in every area, whether hidden alcoholism, perversion, surgical blunders, or engineering mistakes, they merely vary according to the various indirect methods of calculation. But to learn how the seemingly impossible was accomplished, the reader must read the afterword himself.

The new edition also has a new introduction. It is odd. Its author is unquestionably an intellectual who wished to remain anonymous; instead of praising *One Human Minute,* he speaks of it critically and ironically, making one suspect that he considers this numerical fruit of computers collaborating with computers, under human management, to be like the forbidden fruit of the Tree of Knowledge.

He advises against reading the book page by page, for that would be like reading an encyclopedia in alphabetical order—it would only make the reader's head swim. Moreover, he says that he himself, as a reader, was "bullied" by *One Human Minute.* In his opinion, "Everything has always happened at once," because the ineffable *sum* of all humanity's experience is, for every historical instant—for every minute or second—a quantity that is *constant*. The reasons for the cares, joys, and sorrows may change radically, but they do not affect that existential sum. That is the Constant. And even if it shows historical fluctuation, there is no way to discover when an increase in misery takes place and a decrease in pleasure, or vice versa. But the book is valuable as a *background* enabling us to understand what the mass media are telling us as they advance technologically and carry more and more trivia. The image of the book's "ideal reader" is ridiculous; according to the author of the Introduction, such a reader would study it bit by bit, to the exclusion of all else, attempting to glimpse the human reality behind the numbers. The example the author uses to illustrate his ideal reader is ironic; the manipulating of figures almost caricatures the method that gave rise to the whole volume. This ideal reader, having the best of intentions, will power, imagination, and loads of free time, does nothing his whole life long (apart from catching a few hours' sleep) except study what is taking place, at that moment, among his fellow creatures. Devoting thirty seconds to each living person for eighteen hours a day for fifty years, he will be able to contemplate thirty-six million people, but that is not even one two-hundredth of his contemporaries. He will not have time to consider the remaining 199/200 of humanity even if he does nothing else until his dying breath, even if he considers while he eats, drinks, and undresses for bed. This example demonstrates that in reality we can know almost nothing of human fortunes beyond what is given by the statistical data.

The editors, I'm sure, allowed such a skeptical and agnostic introduction, knowing that they had a best seller, because with best sellers condemnation as well as praise increases sales. A cynical observation, perhaps, but true.

Naturally, pirate editions and imitations of *One Human Minute* have appeared. It will be amusing and fitting if the next edition includes phenomena of this sort under the headings

"Intellectual Theft" and "Counterfeiting of Information"; the once-innocent appearance of a best seller now produces a train of imitators—a pack of jackals and hyenas following a lion. Meanwhile, computer crime has moved from fantasy into reality. A bank can indeed be robbed by remote control, with electronic impulses that break or fool security codes, much as a safecracker uses a skeleton key, crowbar, or carborundum saw. Presumably, banks suffer serious losses in this way, but here *One Human Minute* is silent, because—again, presumably—the world of High Finance does not want to make such losses public, fearing to expose this new Achilles' heel: the electronic sabotage of automated bookkeeping. Therefore there is no heading in the book for computer crime, but it is bound to show up sooner or later, in a future edition.

Since the copyright covers the title of the book but not the idea that gave birth to it, one can now find, in the bookstores, *The World Now, What's Happening, Fantastic Reality/Real Fantasy*—which have slightly modified figures in the decimal places, so that the publisher of *One Human Minute* would have difficulty in court in the event of a plagiarism suit. All these imitations, of course, are cut from the same cloth; only once, as I was turning the pages of one of them, did I come upon an introduction that was rather original. The mass media, it said, are never completely objective. In fact, the pattern is like this: the worse the news in the local press, the more freedom there is and the better conditions are in the society that prints it. If journalists are wringing their hands, tearing their hair, predicting the end, and bewailing imminent ruin, then the streets are rivers of glistening cars, the store windows are packed with delicacies, everyone walks around tanned and rosy-cheeked, and a handcuffed wretch brought to prison at gunpoint is harder to find than a diamond in the gutter. And vice versa: where prisons are overcrowded, where gloom and fear prevail, where poverty is terrible, one usually reads—in the papers—news that is cheerful, uplifting, determinedly joyous (telling you that you had better participate in the general happiness), and syrupy press releases paint life in rainbow colors (except that it is a rainbow that *will* shine—but not just yet). This introduction claims an important role for *One Human Minute* and its imitators: to supply the *complete truth*.

The original *One Human Minute* is supposed to be computerized, so that one can call it up on one's home computer. But most people will prefer the volume on the shelf. And so the book, styling itself "all books in one," will increase the mass of printed paper. In it you can find out how many trees fall per minute to saw and ax all over the world. Forests are turned into paper to make newspapers that call for the forests to be saved. But that piece of information is not in *One Human Minute*. You have to figure it out yourself.

## III

Now *One Human Minute* has indeed been computerized, but not in the way I imagined. The fact is, the contents of the book were becoming, slowly but surely, anachronistic. The number of people in the world keeps increasing; new catastrophes and calamities are added to the old ones; new means of production create different articles for daily consumption. Therefore, as in the case of yearly almanacs, it came time to revise the book— or rather, to recalculate it from scratch. But a character appeared, even cleverer than the Johnsons; he decided to put a perpetual *One Human Minute* on the market—valid from year to year—like a perpetual calendar! In an era of pocket calculators, electronic chessplayers, and a host of similar devices claiming to embody "artificial intelligence" (which has not been attained yet but someday, no doubt, will be), when you can buy even a pocket translator to carry on simple conversations in a foreign language, it was possible to make an electronic version of this book, avoiding the need for continual corrections and new editions.

The year is entered, the subject code selected from the menu. Also, one can move both forward and backward in time. Naturally, seeing that the machine can show how many children were born thirty years ago, and how many three hundred years ago, a person is tempted to give it a tougher problem: how many people watched television when Columbus discovered America? The machine is not that stupid, however, and is not taken in. The answer that appears in the little window is "0." We are soon convinced that the past has all been entered in the memory of this new, microcomputerized version of *One Human Minute*. But it is more interesting to use it to look at the future. You cannot jump more than one hundred years forward: when you try, you get an "E" in the little window, signaling overload, as in any ordinary calculator. Future data are extrapolations, derived from such weighty mathematics that I wouldn't dream of going into it. The only thing certain is that all the data are uncertain, like any statement about the future. But since *The Perpetual Human Minute* is really not a book, the book reviewer has no further obligation to it; there remains for him only this parting, possibly profound remark:

In the Holy Scriptures it is said that in the beginning was the Word, and the Word was with God. Paraphrasing for our earthly use, we can observe that in the beginning was a computer, which brought forth this book, which became a computer again. An accident, perhaps, a superficial analogy—but I am afraid that it is not.

# THE UPSIDE-DOWN
# EVOLUTION

## I

Having gained access (by what means, I'm not at liberty to reveal) to several volumes on the military history of the twenty-first century, I pondered, first and foremost, how to hide the information they contained. The question of concealment was most important, because I understood that the man who knew this history was like the finder of a treasure who, defenseless, could easily lose it along with his life. I alone possessed these facts, I realized, thanks to the books that Dr. R.G. loaned to me briefly and which I returned just before his premature death. As far as I know, he burned them, thus taking the secret with him to the grave.

Silence seemed the simplest solution: if I kept quiet, I would save my skin. But what a shame, to sit on a thousand and one extraordinary things having to do with the political history of the next century, things opening up completely new horizons in all areas of human life. Take, for example, the astonishing reversal—completely unforeseen—in the field of artificial intelligence (AI), which became a force to be reckoned with precisely because it did *not* become the machine embodiment of the human mind. If I remained silent for my own safety, I would be depriving myself of all the advantages stemming from that knowledge.

Another idea occurred to me: to write down exactly what I remembered of those volumes and place the manuscript in a bank vault. It would be necessary to write down everything I retained from my reading, because with the passage of time I would forget many particulars of such a broad subject. Then, if I wanted to refresh my memory, I could visit the vault, take notes there, and return the manuscript to the strongbox. But it was dangerous. Someone could spy on me. Besides, in today's world no bank vault was 100-percent secure. Even a thief of low intelligence would figure out, sooner or later, what an extraordinary document had fallen into his hands. And even if he discarded and destroyed my manuscript, I would not know it and would live in constant dread that the connection between my person and the history of the twenty-first century would come to light.

My dilemma was how to hide the secret forever but at the same time take advantage of it freely—to hide it from the world but not from myself. After much deliberation, I realized that this could be done very easily. The safest way to conceal a remarkable idea—every word of it true—was to publish it as science fiction. Just as a diamond thrown on a heap of broken glass would become invisible, so an authentic revelation placed amid the stupidities of science fiction would take on their coloration—and cease to be dangerous.

At first, however, still fearful, I made a very modest use of the secret I possessed. In 1967 I wrote a science-fiction novel entitled *His Master's Voice* (published in English in 1983 by Harcourt Brace Jovanovich). On page 125 of that edition, third line from the top, are the words "the ruling doctrine was . . . 'indirect economic attrition,'" and then the doctrine is expressed by the aphorism "The thin starve before the fat lose weight."

The doctrine expressed publicly in the United States in 1980—thirteen years after the original edition of *His Master's Voice*—was put a little differently. (In the West German press they used the slogan *"den Gegner totrüsten"*—"arm the enemy to death.")

Once I had confirmed—and there had been time enough to do so, after all, since the book's appearance—that no one had noticed how my "fantasizing" agreed with later political developments, I grew bolder. I understood that truth, when set in fiction, is camouflaged perfectly, and that even this fact can be safely confessed. For that matter, no one takes anything seriously if it's published. So the best way to keep a top secret secret is to put it out in a mass edition.

Having ensured the safety of my secret thus, I can now serenely set about giving a complete report. I will confine myself to the first two volumes of *Weapons Systems of the Twenty-first Century: The Upside-down Evolution,* published in 2105. I could even name the authors (none of whom has been born yet), but what would be the point? The work is in three volumes. The first presents the development of weapons from the year 1944; the second explains how the nuclear-arms race gave rise to the "unhumanizing" of warfare by transferring the production of weapons from the defense industry to the battlefield itself; and the third deals with the effect this greatest military revolution had on the subsequent history of the world.

## II

Soon after the destruction of Hiroshima and Nagasaki, American nuclear researchers founded the *Bulletin of the Atomic Scientists.* On its cover they put the picture of a clock with the minute hand at ten to midnight. Six years later, after the first successful tests of the hydrogen bomb, they moved the hand five minutes closer, and when the Soviet Union acquired thermonuclear weapons the hand was moved three minutes closer. The next move would mean the end of civilization. The *Bulletin*'s doctrine was "One World or None": the world would either unite and be saved, or would perish.

With the nuclear build-up on both sides of the ocean and the placing of ever larger payloads of plutonium and tritium in ever more accurate ballistic missiles, none of the scientists who were the "fathers of the bomb" believed that peace—troubled as it was by local, conventional wars—would last to the end of the century. Atomic weapons had amended Clausewitz's famous definition ("War is . . . a continuation of political activity by other means"), because now the threat of attack could substitute for the attack itself. Thus came about the doctrine of symmetrical deterrence known later as the "balance of terror." Different American administrations advocated it with different initials. There was, for example, MAD (Mutual Assured Destruction), based on the "second-strike" principle (the ability of the country attacked to retaliate in force). The vocabulary of destruction was enriched in the next decades. There was "Total Strategic Exchange," meaning all-out nuclear war; MIRV (Multiple Independently Targetable Re-entry Vehicle), a missile firing a number of warheads simultaneously, each aimed at a different target; PENAID (Penetration Aids), dummy missiles to fool the opponent's radar; and MARY (Maneuverable Re-entry), a missile capable of evading antimissiles and of hitting the target within fifty feet of the programmed "ground zero." But to list even a hundredth of the succession of specialized terms is impossible here.

Although the danger of atomic warfare increased whenever "equality" was lessened, and therefore the rational thing would seem to have been to preserve that equality under multinational supervision, the antagonists did not reach an agreement despite repeated negotiations.

There were many reasons, which the authors of *Weapons Systems* divide into two groups. In the first group they see the pressure of traditional thinking in international politics. Tradition has determined that one should call for peace but prepare for war, upsetting the existing balance until the upper hand is gained. The second group of reasons are factors independent of human thought both political and nonpolitical; these have to do with the evolution of the major applied military technologies.

Each new possibility of technological improvement in weaponry became a reality, on the principle "If we don't do it, they will." Meanwhile, the doctrine of nuclear warfare went through changes. At one time it advocated a limited exchange of nuclear strikes (though no one knew exactly what the guarantee of the limitation would be); at another, its goal was the *total* annihilation of the enemy (all of whose population became "hostages" of a sort); at still another, it gave first priority to destroying the enemy's military-industrial potential.

The ancient law of "sword and shield" still held sway in the evolution of weaponry. The shield took the form of hardening the silos that housed the missiles, while the sword to pierce the shield involved making the missiles increasingly accurate and, later, providing them with self-guidance systems and self-maneuverability. For atomic submarines the shield was the ocean; improved methods for their underwater detection constituted the sword.

Technological progress in defense sent electronic "eyes" into orbit, creating a high frontier of global reconnaissance able to spot missiles at the moment of launch. This was the shield that the new type of sword—the "killer satellite"—was to break, with a laser to blind the defending "eyes," or with a lightninglike discharge of immense power to destroy the missiles themselves during their flight above the atmosphere.

41

But the hundreds of billions of dollars invested in building these higher and higher levels of conflict failed, ultimately, to produce any definite, and therefore valuable, strategic advantage —and for two very different, almost unrelated reasons.

In the first place, all these improvements and innovations, instead of increasing strategic security, offensive or defensive, only reduced it. Security was reduced because the global system of each superpower grew more and more complex, composed of an increasing number of different subsystems on land, sea, and air and in space. Military success required infallible communications to guarantee the optimum synchronization of operations. But all systems that are highly complex, whether they be industrial or military, biological or technological, whether they process information or raw material, are prone to breakdown, to a degree mathematically proportional to the number of elements that make up the system. Progress in military technology carried with it a unique paradox: the more sophisticated the weapon it produced, the greater was the role of chance (which could not be calculated) in the weapon's successful use.

This fundamental problem must be explained carefully, because scientists were for a long time unable to base any technological activity on the randomness of complex systems. To counteract malfunctions in such systems, engineers introduced redundancy: power reserves, for example, or—as with the first American space shuttles (like the Columbia)—the doubling, even quadrupling of parallel, onboard computers. Total reliability is unattainable: if a system has a million elements and each element will malfunction only one time out of a million, a breakdown is *certain*.

The bodies of animals and plants consist of trillions of functioning parts, yet life copes with the phenomenon of inevitable failure. In what way? The experts call it the construction of reliable systems out of unreliable components. Natural evolution uses various tactics to counteract the fallibility of organisms:

42

the capacity for self-repair or regeneration; surplus organs (this is why we have two kidneys instead of one, why a half-destroyed liver can still function as the body's central chemical-processing plant, and why the circulatory system has so many alternate veins and arteries); and the separation of control centers for the somatic and psychic processes. This last phenomenon gave brain researchers much trouble: they could not understand why a seriously injured brain still functioned but a slightly damaged computer refused to obey its programs.

Merely doubling control centers and parts used in twentieth-century engineering led to the absurd in actual construction. If an automated spaceship going to a distant planet were built according to the directive of multiplying pilot computers, as in the shuttles, then it would have to contain—in view of the duration of the flight—not four or five but possibly fifty such computers. They would operate not by "linear logic" but by "voting": once the individual computers ceased functioning identically and thus diverged in their results, one would have to accept, as the right result, what was reached by the majority. But this kind of engineering parliamentarianism led to the production of giants burdened with the woes typical of democracies: contradictory views, plans, and actions. To such pluralism, to such programmed *elasticity*, there had to be a limit.

We should have begun much earlier—said the twenty-first-century specialists—to learn from biological evolution, whose several-billion-year existence demonstrates optimal strategic engineering. A living organism is not guided by "totalitarian centralism" or "democratic pluralism," but by a strategy much more complex. Simplifying, we might call it a compromise between concentration and separation of the regulating centers.

Meanwhile, in the late-twentieth-century phase of the arms race, the role of unpredictable chance increased. When hours (or days) and miles (or hundreds of miles) separate defeat from victory, and therefore an error of command can be remedied by throwing in reserves, or retreating, or counterattacking, then there is room to reduce the element of chance. But when micromillimeters and nanoseconds determine the outcome, then chance enters like a god of war, deciding victory or defeat; it is magnified and lifted out of the microscopic scale of atomic physics. The fastest, best weapons system comes up against the Heisenberg uncertainty principle, which *nothing* can overcome, because that principle is a basic property of matter in the Universe. It need not be a computer breakdown in satellite reconnaissance or in missiles whose warheads parry defenses with laser beams; if a series of electronic defensive impulses is even a billionth of a second slow in meeting a similar series of offensive impulses, that is enough for a toss of the dice to decide the outcome of the Final Encounter.

Unaware of this state of affairs, the major antagonists of the planet devised two opposite strategies. One can call them the "scalpel" and the "hammer." The constant escalation of payload megatonnage was the hammer; the improvement of detection and swift destruction in flight was the scalpel. They also reckoned on the deterrent of the "dead man's revenge": the enemy would realize that even in winning he would perish, since a totally obliterated country would still respond—automatically and posthumously—with a strike that would make defeat universal. Such was the direction the arms race was taking, and such was its destination, which no one wanted but no one knew how to avoid.

How does the engineer minimize error in a very large, very complex system? He does trial runs to test it; he looks for weak spots, weak links. But there was no way of testing a system designed to wage global nuclear war, a system made up of surface, submarine, air-launched, and satellite missiles, antimissiles, and multiple centers of command and communications, ready to loose gigantic destructive forces in wave on wave of reciprocal atomic strikes. No maneuvers, no computer simulation, could re-create the actual conditions of such a battle.

Increasing speed of operation marked each new weapons system, particularly the decision-making function (to strike or not to strike, where, how, with what force held in reserve, at what risk, etc.), and this increasing speed also brought the incalculable factor of chance into play. Lightning-fast systems made lightning-fast mistakes. When a fraction of a second determined the safety or destruction of a region, a great metropolis, an industrial complex, or a large fleet, it was impossible to achieve military certainty. One could even say that victory had ceased to be distinguishable from defeat. In a word, the arms race was heading toward a Pyrrhic situation.

On the battlefields of yore, when knights in armor fought on horseback and foot soldiers met at close quarters, chance decided the life or death of individuals and military units. But the power of electronics, embodied in computer logic, made chance the arbiter of the fate of whole armies and nations.

Moreover—and this was quite a separate thing—blueprints for new, better weapons were developed so quickly that industry could not keep pace. Control systems, targeting systems, camouflage, maintenance and disruption of communications, the strike capability of so-called conventional weapons (a misleading term, really, and out of date) became anachronisms even before they were put into the field.

That is why, in the late eighties, production was frequently halted on new fighter planes and bombers, cruise missiles, anti-antimissiles, spy satellites, submarines, laser bombs, sonars, and radars. That is why prototypes had to be abandoned and why so much political debate seethed around successive weapons that swallowed huge budgets and vast human energies. Not only did each innovation turn out to be far more expensive than the one before, but many soon had to be written off as losses, and this pattern continued without letup. It seemed that technological-military invention *per se* was not the answer, but, rather, the speed of its industrial implementation. This phenomenon became, at the turn of the century, the latest paradox of the arms race. The only way to nullify its awful drain on the military appeared to be to plan weapons not eight or twelve years ahead, but a quarter of a century in advance—which was a sheer impossibility, requiring the prediction of new discoveries and inventions beyond the ken of the best minds of the day.

At the end of the twentieth century, the idea emerged of a new weapon that would be neither an atom bomb nor a laser gun but a hybrid of the two. Up to then, there were fission (uranium, plutonium) and fusion (thermonuclear, hydrogen-plutonium) bombs. The "old" bomb, in breaking nuclear bonds, unleashed every possible sort of radiation: gamma rays, X-rays, heat, and an avalanche of radioactive dust and lethal high-energy particles. The fireball, having a temperature of millions of degrees, emitted energy at all wavelengths. As someone said, "Matter vomited forth everything she could." From a military standpoint it was wasteful, because at ground zero all objects turned into flaming plasma, a gas of atoms stripped of their electron shells. At the site of the explosion, stones, trees, houses, metals, bridges, and human bodies vaporized, and concrete and sand were hurled into the stratosphere in a rising mushroom of flames. "Conversion bombs" were a more efficient version of this weapon. They emitted what the strategists required in a given situation: either hard radiation—in which case it was called a "clean bomb," striking only living things—or thermal radiation, which unleashed a firestorm over hundreds of square miles.

The laser bomb, however, was not actually a bomb; it was a single-charge laser gun, focusing a huge part of its force into a ray that could incinerate a city (from a high orbit), for example, or a rocket base, or some other important target (such as the enemy's satellite defense screen). At the same time, the ray would turn the laser bomb itself into flaming fragments. But we will not go into more detail about such weapons, because instead of leading to further escalation, as was expected, they really marked its end.

It is worthwhile, however, to look at the atomic arsenals of twentieth-century Earth from a historical perspective. Even in the seventies, they held enough weapons to kill every inhabitant of the planet several times over. Given this overabundance of destructive might, the specialists favored a preventive strike, or making a second strike at the enemy's stockpiles while protecting their own. The safety of the population was important but second in priority.

In the early fifties, the *Bulletin of the Atomic Scientists* printed a discussion in which the fathers of the bomb, physicists like Bethe and Szilard, took part. It dealt with civil defense in the event of nuclear war. A realistic solution would have meant evacuating the cities and building gigantic underground shelters. Bethe estimated the cost of the first phase of such a project to be twenty billion dollars, though the social and psychological costs were beyond reckoning. But it soon became clear that even a "return to the cave" would not guarantee the survival of the population, because the arms race continued to yield more powerful warheads and increasingly accurate missiles. The science fiction of the day painted gloomy and nightmarish scenes in which the degenerate remnants of humanity vegetated in concrete, multilevel molehills beneath the ruins of gutted cities. Self-styled futurologists (but all futurologists were self-styled) outdid one another in extrapolating, from existing atomic arsenals, future arsenals even more frightful. One of the better known of such speculations was Herman Kahn's *Thinking about the Unthinkable*, an essay on hydrogen warfare. Kahn also thought up a "doomsday machine." An enormous nuclear charge encased in a cobalt jacket could be buried by a nation in the depths of its own territory, in order to blackmail the rest of the world with the threat of "total planetary suicide." But no one dreamed that, with political antagonisms still persisting, the era of atomic weapons would come to an end without ushering in either world peace or world annihilation.

During the early years of the twenty-first century, theoretical physics pondered a question that was thought to be crucial for the world's continued existence: namely, whether or not the critical mass of uranides like uranium 235 and plutonium (that is, the mass at which an initiated chain reaction causes a nuclear explosion) was an *absolute* constant. If the critical mass could be influenced, particularly at a great distance, there might be a chance of neutralizing all warheads. As it turned out (and the physicists of the previous century had a rough idea of this), the critical mass *could* change. Under certain physical conditions, an explosive charge that had been critical ceased to be critical, and therefore did not explode. But the amount of energy needed to create such conditions was far greater than the power contained in all the atomic weapons combined. These attempts to neutralize atomic weapons were unsuccessful.

## III

In the 1990s a new type of missile, popularly called the "F&F" (Fire & Forget), made its appearance. Guided by a programmed microcomputer, the missile sought its own target after being launched. Once activated, it was truly on its own. At the same time, "unhuman" espionage came into use, at first underwater. An underwater mine, equipped with sensors and memory, could keep track of the movements of ships sailing over it, distinguish commercial vessels from military, establish their tonnage, and transmit the information in code if necessary.

Combat readiness, in the affluent nations especially, evaporated. Young men of draft age considered such time-honored phrases as *Dulce et decorum est pro patria mori* to be completely ridiculous.

Meanwhile, new generations of weapons were rising in price exponentially. The airplane of the First World War was made of canvas, wood, and piano wire, with a couple of machine guns; landing gear and all, it cost about as much as a good automobile. A comparable airplane of the Second World War cost as much as thirty automobiles. By the end of the century, the price of a jet interceptor or a radar-proof bomber of the "Stealth" type was in the hundreds of millions of dollars. Aircraft for the year 2000 were expected to cost a billion apiece. At this rate, it was calculated that over the next eighty years each superpower would be able to afford only twenty to twenty-five new planes. Tanks were no cheaper. And an atomic aircraft carrier, which was like an antediluvian brontosaurus under fire, cost many billions. The carrier could be sunk by a single hit from an F&F superrocket, which could split over the target into a cluster of specialized warheads, each to strike at a different nerve center of the sea leviathan.

At this same time, the production of microchips was discontinued; they were replaced by a product of the latest genetic engineering. The strain *Silocobacter wieneri* (named after the creator of cybernetics, Norbert Wiener) produced, in solutions containing silicates, silver, and a secret ingredient, solid-state circuits that were smaller than fly's eggs. These elements were called "grain," and after four years of mass production a handful of them cost no more than a handful of corn. In this way, from the intersection of two curves—the rising curve of cost for heavy weaponry and the falling curve of cost for artificial intelligence —came the "unhumanization" of the military.

Armies began to change from living to nonliving forces. Initially, the effects of the change were undramatic. It was like the automobile, whose inventors did not immediately come up with an entirely new shape but, instead, simply put an internal-combustion engine in a cart or carriage, with the harness removed. Similarly, the earliest pioneers of aviation gave their flying machines the wings of birds. Thanks to this kind of mental inertia, which in the military is considerable, not very radical new missiles, unmanned tanks, and self-propelled artillery were adapted for the new microsilicon "soldier," simply by reducing them in size and installing computer-controlled command modules. But this was anachronistic. The new, nonliving microsoldier required a whole new approach to tactics, strategy, and, of course, to the question of what *kinds* of weapons he could put to best use.

This came at a time when the world was slowly recovering from two economic crises. The first was caused by the formation of the OPEC cartel and the big increases in the price of crude oil; the second, by the collapse of OPEC and the sudden drop in the price of oil. Although early nuclear-power plants were in operation, they were of no use for powering land or air vehicles. This is why the cost of heavy equipment such as troop carriers, artillery, missiles, trucks, tanks, and submarines, not to mention the cost of the newer (late-twentieth-century) types of heavy weapons, was constantly on the rise, even though by then the troop carriers had no one to transport and before long the artillery would have no one to shell.

This final phase of the military's gigantomania in weaponry gave way to a period of microminiaturization under the banner of artificial *nonintelligence*. Oddly enough, it was only in 2040 that the informationists, cipher theorists, and other experts expressed surprise at how their predecessors could have been so blind for so long, struggling to create artificial intelligence. After all, for the overwhelming majority of tasks performed by people in 97.8 percent of both blue- and white-collar jobs, intelligence was not necessary. What *was* necessary? A command of the situation, skill, care, and enterprise. All these qualities are found in insects.

A wasp of the Sphecidae family finds herself a cricket and

injects into its nervous system a poison that paralyzes but does not kill. Next she digs a burrow in the sand, sets her victim beside it, enters the burrow to make sure that it is usable—free of dampness or ants—then drags the cricket inside, deposits her egg in it, and flies off to repeat the process. The wasp's larva will feed on the living body of the cricket until the larva changes into a pupa. The wasp thus displays an excellent command of the situation in the choice of victim and in the anesthetic procedure she performs on it; skill in preparing an enclosure for it; care in checking the enclosure to see that conditions are suitable for her offspring; and enterprise, without which this whole series of activities could never have been carried through.

The wasp may have enough nerve tissue to drive a truck from a port to a distant city or to guide a transcontinental rocket. It is only that its nervous system was programmed by natural evolution for completely different tasks.

Successive generations of information theorists and computer scientists had labored in vain to imitate the functions of the human brain in computers; stubbornly they ignored a mechanism a million times simpler than the brain, incredibly small, and remarkably reliable in its operation. Not *artificial intelligence* but *artificial instinct* should have been simulated for programming at the outset. Instinct appeared almost a billion years earlier than intelligence—clear proof that it is easier to produce.

From studying the neurology and neuroanatomy of the mindless insect the specialists of the mid-twenty-first century quickly obtained splendid results. Their predecessors were truly blind to overlook the fact that such insects as bees, seemingly primitive creatures, nevertheless possess their own, inherited language, with which the workers in the hive inform one another of the location of newly discovered nectar. Through signal-gesture-pantomime the direction of the path is given, the time required to reach the nectar, and even its relative quantity.

Of course, the point was not to duplicate wasps, flies, spiders, or bees in computer chips or the like; the important thing was their neural anatomy with its built-in sequences of directed behavior and programmed goals. The result was a scientific-technological revolution that totally and irreversibly transformed the battlegrounds of Earth. Until then, all arms had been fashioned to fit man; their components were tailored to his anatomy, so that he could kill effectively, and to his physiology, so that he could be killed effectively.

As so often happened, the beginnings of this complex new trend lay in the twentieth century, but at that time no one was able to combine them into a novel synthesis, because the discoveries that made possible the unhumanization of weapons systems took place in widely separated fields. Military experts had no interest in insects (except the lice, fleas, and other parasites that beset soldiers in wartime). Intellectronics engineers, who with the entomologists and neurologists studied the neurology of insects, knew nothing about military problems. And politicians, true to form, knew nothing about anything.

Thus, while intellectronics was developing microcalculators so small that they competed in size with the nerve bundles of mosquitoes and hornets, the majority of artificial-intelligence enthusiasts were still busy programming computers to carry on stupid conversations with not-too-bright people. The mammoths and dinosaurs of the computer species were beating chess masters not because they were more intelligent but only because they could process data a billion times faster than Einstein. For a long time no one imagined that all the ordinary front-line soldier needed was the skill and enterprise of a bee or a hornet. In basic military operations, intelligence and combat effectiveness are two entirely different things. (Intelligence can actually be a negative factor. In battle, the soldier's instinct for self-preservation, incomparably greater than a bee's, can *interfere;* the bee, on the other hand, will sting to defend its hive though the sting means its own death.) Who knows how long the old-fashioned way of thinking would have continued in the weapons industry—the search for new conventional and unconventional instruments of warfare, the spiraling arms race—had it not been for a few works that directed the public's attention to a remote and unusual episode in our planet's history.

## IV

Sixty-five million years ago, on the so-called C-T geological boundary (between the Cretaceous and the Tertiary), a meteorite fell on our planet. It had a diameter of about ten kilometers and contained a considerable amount of iron and iridium. Its mass is estimated to have been over three and a half trillion (3,600,000,000,000) tons. It is unclear whether it was one mass, hence an asteroid from the region between Earth and Mars, or a group of bodies forming the head of a comet. In the geological stratum of this period, iridium and rare earth metals have been discovered in amounts and concentrations not normally found in the Earth's crust. The absence of an impact crater made it difficult to prove the planetary scale of this cataclysm, since craters that appeared later (caused by meteorites a thousand times smaller) left marks on the Earth's surface that are clearly visible today. Most likely, this asteroid or comet did not strike any of the continents but landed in the open ocean—or else the collision took place near a junction of continental plates, and the subsequent shifting obliterated the crater.

A meteor of such size and mass can easily pass through the protective layer of the atmosphere. The energy of the impact, comparable in magnitude to the energy of all the world's nuclear stockpiles (if not larger), turned that body—or group of bodies —into thousands of billions of tons of dust, which the air currents spread over the entire surface of the Earth, creating a cloud so thick and long-lasting that for at least four months photosynthesis ceased in plants on all continents. Darkness reigned; the land surface, no longer heated by the sun's rays, grew much colder than did the ocean, which cooled more slowly. Nevertheless, the marine algae, one of the main sources of atmospheric oxygen, also lost their ability to carry on photosynthesis during that time. As a result, an enormous number of plant and animal species became extinct. The most spectacular extinction was that of the giant reptiles commonly called dinosaurs—although at least several hundred other reptile species died out then, too. The catastrophe occurred at a time when the Earth's climate was gradually cooling, and the large, hairless Mesozoic reptiles found themselves in great difficulty. Even before the cataclysm, their viability had been on the wane for about a million years, as the fossil record reveals. The calcium shells of the dinosaur eggs grew thinner as the millennia passed—testimony to the increasing hardships in feeding and to the worsening climate of the large landmasses.

Computer simulations of such an event, done back in the 1980s, verified its lethal effect on the biosphere. Strangely enough, the phenomenon to which we owe our emergence as a rational species was not introduced into any school curriculum, even though there was not the slightest doubt about the connection between the Cretaceous-Tertiary saurocide and anthropogenesis.

Paleontological research toward the end of the twentieth century proved that the dinosaurs were warm-blooded, and that the winged varieties were covered with something very much like feathers. The mammal species that coexisted with these reptiles, having no opportunity to evolve, did not exceed the size of a rat or a squirrel. Competition on land, in the water, and in the air from the powerful, hardy reptiles was too great; the mammals were but an evolutionary footnote to the carnivorous and herbivorous vertebrates of the day.

The planetary catastrophe worked against the large animals

not directly but indirectly, through the interruption of the food chain in the biosphere. When photosynthesis stopped, vegetation withered on a massive scale, and the large herbivorous reptiles of land, sea, and air could not find enough food. The predators who ate the herbivores perished for the same reason. A huge number of marine animals also died out, because in the oceans the biological carbon cycle proceeds much faster than on land, and because the surface layers of water cooled more quickly than the deeper layers. A few small reptile species did survive. But the small mammal survivors were numerous, and so, when the dust of the meteor settled and the atmosphere cleared and plant life revived, they began to differentiate, branching into many species, which after forty million years produced the line of primates from which *Homo sapiens* descended.

Thus the cause—indirect but undoubted—of rational man's emergence was a cataclysm on the C-T boundary. For our subject, however—the military evolution of civilization—it is the consequences of this event, so long overlooked, that are important. The fact is that the ones who suffered least on the C-T boundary were the insects! Before the catastrophe there were about three-quarters of a million insect species; a short time afterward, there were still at least seven hundred thousand, and social insects like ants, termites, and bees survived the cataclysm practically unimpaired. This leads us to conclude that cataclysms are survived most easily and with the greatest probability by small or very small animals with an insectile anatomy and physiology.

Nor should one consider it an accident that insects are generally much less susceptible to the lethal effects of radioactivity than the so-called higher animals, the vertebrates. Paleontology speaks unequivocally. A catastrophe that unleashed the destructive force of a global atomic war killed every one of the large animals but did little damage to the insects and did not touch the bacteria. This shows that the greater the destructive action of an elemental force or technological weapon, the smaller must a system be in order to survive it unharmed. Thus the atomic bomb demanded the dispersal not only of whole armies but also of *individual soldiers*. General staffs considered dispersing their armies, but in the twentieth century the idea of reducing a soldier to the size of an ant or a wasp found no expression outside the pages of fantasy. A human being couldn't be reduced or dispersed! In those days much thought was given to soldier-automatons—humanoid robots—a naïve anthropomorphism. Yet heavy industry was already undergoing unhumanization, and the robots that replaced people on the assembly lines were not remotely humanoid. They were the enlargement of selected, functional *parts* of the human being: a computer "brain" with one huge steel hand assembling a car chassis, or a system with a hammer-fist, or with a laser-finger to weld the bodies. These devices worked like eyes and hands but did not look like eyes or hands. But large and heavy robots such as these could not be put on the battlefield, where they would immediately become the target of accurate, self-guided, intelligent missiles.

So it was not humanoid automata that formed the new armies but synthetic insects (synsects)—ceramic microcrustacea, titanium annelids, and flying pseudo-hymenoptera with nerve centers made of arsenic compounds and with stingers of heavy, fissionable elements. Most of this "nonliving micropersonnel" could, at the first warning of an atomic attack, dig deep into the ground and then crawl out after the explosion, maintaining combat functions even in an environment glowing with terrible radioactivity, because these soldiers were not only microscopic but nonbiological. The flying synsect combined plane, pilot, and missile in one miniature whole. But the operating unit was the *microarmy*, which possessed superior combat effectiveness only as a whole (just as a colony of bees was an independent, surviving unit while a single bee was nothing).

Because the battlefield was constantly exposed to atomic

attack, which not only destroyed combat forces but also disrupted all communications between the various weapons systems (and also between the weapons and their command centers), there arose nonliving microarmies of many types. These were based on two opposing principles.

According to the first—the principle of *autonomy*—an army proceeded like a column of ants, or a wave of microbes, or a swarm of locusts. The last analogy is particularly apt. The locust, as we know, is simply a biological variety of the common grasshopper (not a separate species); even in clouds numbering hundreds of billions of specimens (still greater numbers have been observed from planes) it is not directly harmful to humans.* Nevertheless, the sheer mass of a locust cloud can cause a train to derail, turn day into night, and paralyze all movement. (Even a tank, entering a cloud of locusts, will begin to slip as it crushes the insects into a pulp of ichor and grease and will bog down as in a quagmire.) The nonliving, synthetic "locust" was incomparably more lethal, since it was made that way by its designers. It possessed a preprogrammed autonomy, so that communication with a command center was unnecessary.

The pseudo-locust could be destroyed, of course, by an atomic attack, but this would have an effect like that of shooting at clouds with nuclear weapons: great holes would open, only to fill again with more cloud.

According to the second principle of the new military—*telotropism*—the microarmy was one giant flowing or flying aggregate of self-assembling elements. It started out dispersed, approaching its objective from many different directions, as strategy or tactics demanded, in order to concentrate into a preprogrammed whole on the battlefield. For this fighting material did not leave the factory in final shape, ready for use, like

*If one disregards the chief destructive result of such visitations—that is, the total loss of vegetation and cultivated crops.

tanks or guns loaded on a railroad flatcar; the mechanisms were microproductive blocks designed to fuse together into a war machine at the designated place. For this reason, such armies were called "self-bonding."

The simplest example was a self-dispersing atomic weapon. Any missile launched from land, ship, or submarine could be destroyed from space by a satellite laser. But it was impossible to destroy gigantic clouds of microparticles carrying uranium or plutonium that merged into a critical mass only at the target. En route to the target, they were so dispersed as to be indistinguishable from fog or dust.

The competition between old and new weapons was brief: massive, armored equipment could not withstand the attacks of the microarmies. Just as germs invisibly invade an organism to kill it from within, so the nonliving, artificial microbes, following the tropisms built into them, penetrated the gun barrels, cartridge chambers, tank and plane engines. They corroded the metal catalytically, or, reaching the powder charges or fuel tanks, blew them up. What could even the bravest soldier, carrying grenades, a machine gun, a bazooka, or any other firearm, do against a nonliving, microscopic enemy? He would be like a doctor trying to fight the bacteria of cholera with a hammer or a revolver.

Amid a swarm of self-guided, programmed microarms, a man in uniform was as helpless as a Roman legionary with sword and shield against a hail of bullets. In the face of special types of biotropic microarms capable of destroying everything that lived, human beings had no choice but to abandon the battlefield, for they would be killed in seconds.

Even in the twentieth century, the tactic of fighting in close ranks gave way to the spreading of troops, and in a mobile war the spreading was still greater. But the front lines still existed, separating friend from foe. Now such boundaries disappeared completely.

A microarmy could easily penetrate all systems of defense and go deep into enemy territory. It had no more trouble accomplishing this than did rain or snow. Meanwhile, high-powered nuclear weapons were proving more and more useless on the battlefield. Imagine, if you will, an attempt to combat a virus epidemic with thermonuclear bombs. It was possible, of course, to scorch a large territory down to a depth of fifty feet, turning it into a vitrified, lifeless desert. But what good was that if on that expanse, one hour later, a military rain began to fall and from it there crystallized detachments of shock troops? Hydrogen bombs were expensive. One didn't hunt in warships for leeches or sardines.

The greatest problem in the unhuman stage of military history was that of distinguishing friend from foe. This task had been accomplished, in the twentieth century, by means of electronic systems working on a password principle. Challenged by radio, a plane or an unmanned missile either radioed the right answer or else was attacked as an enemy craft. This ancient method now proved useless. The new weapon-makers again borrowed from the biosphere—from plants, bacteria, and insects.

Recognition duplicated the methods of identification used among living species: their immunology—the struggle of antigen with antibody—tropisms, protective coloration, camouflage, and mimicry. The nonliving weapon might imitate (extremely well) floating dust specks or pollen, or gnats, or drops of water. But under that mask lay a corrosive or lethal agent.

It should be pointed out that although I am using metaphors from entomology in talking about attacks of artificial locusts or other insects, I do so as a twentieth-century person would describe, to the contemporaries of Vasco Da Gama or Christopher Columbus, a modern city with its automobile traffic. He would speak of carriages and wagons without horses; he would compare airplanes to birds made of metal. In this way he would evoke in the minds of his listeners images that had some connection with reality, albeit an imperfect one. A carriage rolling on large, thin wheels, with high little doors and a dropped step, with a box for the coachman and places at the back for the servants, is not a Fiat or a Mercedes. By the same token, the twenty-first-century synsect weapon is not a swarm of insects just like the ones in an entomologist's atlas, only made of metal.

Some of the pseudo-insects could pierce the human body like bullets; others could form optical systems to throw sunlight over wide areas, altering the temperature of large air masses so as to produce heavy rainfall or fair weather, according to the needs of the campaign. There existed "meteorological insects" corresponding to nothing we know today. The endothermic synsects, for example, absorbed large quantities of energy for the sole purpose of causing a sudden drop in temperature over a given area, resulting in a thick fog or the phenomenon known as an inversion. Then there were synsects able to concentrate themselves into a single-use laser beamer; they replaced the artillery of the previous century—although one can hardly speak of replacement, since artillery as we understand it would have been of as much use on the battlefield as slings and catapults. New weapons dictated new conditions of combat and, therefore, new strategy and tactics, both totally unhuman.

For those who loved the uniform, the flag, the changing of the guard, standing at attention, drill, medals, and bayonet charges, the new era of war was an affront to their noble ideals, a mockery, a disgrace! The experts of the day called the new military science an "upside-down evolution," because in nature what came first were the simple, microscopic systems, which then changed over the eons into larger and larger life forms. In the military evolution of the postnuclear period, the exact opposite took place: microminiaturization.

The microarmies developed in two stages. In the first stage, the unhumaned microweapons were still designed and built by people. In the second stage, microsoldiers were designed, combat-tested, and sent to be mass-produced by "construction battalions" of nonliving microdesigners.

A phenomenon known as "sociointegrative degeneration" displaced humans first from the military and later from the weapons industry. The individual soldier degenerated when he ceased to be an intelligent being with a large brain and grew increasingly small and therefore increasingly simple, or when he became disposable, a "single-use soldier." (Some of the antimilitarists had maintained, long before, that modern warfare's high mortality rate made "single-use soldiers" of all the combatants, with the exception of the top-ranking officers.) In the end, a microfighter had as much brain as an ant or a termite.

A greater role, then, was assumed by the pseudo-sociointegrative collective of microsoldiers. Each nonliving army was incomparably more complex than a beehive or an anthill. In internal structure and interrelationships it was more akin to an ecological unit in nature—that is, to those pyramids of plant and animal species that coexist in a specific region or habitat in evolutionary equilibrium, with their antagonisms and symbioses forming a complex network of interdependencies.

It is easy to see that in such an army there was nothing for noncommissioned officers to do. A corporal or a sergeant, even a general, could not lead a division of such an army. To grasp the whole picture, as complex as nature itself (although quite dead), the wisdom of a university senate would not have sufficed —even for a mere inspection, much less an actual campaign. Besides the impoverished nations of the Third World, therefore, those who suffered the most from the great military revolution of the twenty-first century were the officer cadres.

The twentieth century had already begun the process of destroying them, dispensing with swords, three-cornered hats, and gorgeous uniforms. The final blow, however, was dealt in the twenty-first century by the army's pseudo-insect evolution—or, rather, *involution*. The cruel pressure to unhumanize the armies did away with the picturesque traditions of war games, the pageantry of parades (a marching locust, unlike a procession of tanks or rockets, is not a grand sight), the bayonet drills, the bugle calls, the flag raisings and lowerings, the roll calls, the whole rich fabric of barracks life. For a time, high-ranking command positions were kept for people, but not for very long.

The strategical-numerical superiority of the computer-produced echelons finally forced even the most competent of commanders, including field marshals, into retirement. A tapestry of ribbons and medals on the chest was no protection against being put out to pasture. In various countries, at that time, a resistance movement developed among career officers. In the desperation of unemployment, they even joined the terrorist underground. It was a malicious trick of history—no one deliberately planned it—that these insurrections were crushed by means of microspies and minipolice built on the model of a particular cockroach.

This roach, first described in 1981 by an eminent American neuroentomologist, has at the end of its abdomen fine hairs that are sensitive to even the slightest stirring in the air. Connected to a special dorsal nerve bundle, the hairs enable the roach to detect the approach of an enemy, even in complete darkness, and so to flee instantly. The counterparts to these hairs were the electronic picosensors of the minipolicemen who concealed themselves in cracks in old wallpaper at the rebel headquarters.

But things were not so good in the affluent nations, either. It was impossible to go on with the old political games. The line between war and peace, increasingly blurred for some time, was now obliterated entirely. The twentieth century had discarded the ritual of formal declarations of war, introducing the sneak attack, the fifth column, mass sabotage, cold war, and war by proxy, but this was only the beginning of the erosion of distinctions.

A world with two mutually exclusive political conditions—war or peace—changed into a world in which war was peace and peace became war. In the past, when covert agents were all human beings, they hid their mischief behind various masks of respectability and virtue. They infiltrated religious and social movements, including even senior citizens' choral societies and organizations of matchbox collectors. Later, however, anything could be a covert agent: a nail in the wall, a laundry detergent. Military espionage and sabotage flourished. Since human beings were no longer a real political or military force, there was no point in winning them over with propaganda or in talking them into collaborating with the enemy. Unable to write here about the political changes as much as they warrant, I will convey in a few words the essence of what took place.

Even in the previous century the politicians of the parliamentary countries could not keep up with everything that was going on in their own countries—much less in the world—and so they had advisers. Every political party had its experts. But the advisers of the different parties said completely different things. With time, computer systems were brought in to help; too late, people realized they were becoming the mouthpieces of their computers. They thought *they* were the ones doing the reasoning, drawing independent conclusions based on data supplied by computer memory; but in fact they were operating with material preprocessed by the computer centers, and that material was determining human decisions.

After a period of some confusion, the major parties concluded that the expert advisers were dispensable middlemen; from then on, each party headquarters had a main computer. In the second half of the twenty-first century, when a party took power its computer was sometimes given the post of minister without portfolio (a computer did not need a portfolio anyway), and the pivotal role in such democracies was played by programmers. The programmer took a loyalty oath, but that did not prove very effective. Democracy, many warned, was becoming computerocracy.

For this reason, too, espionage and counterespionage turned away from politicians and environmental-protection groups (of which there were few, since by then there was not much left to save) and infiltrated the computation and decision centers. Of course, no one could absolutely prove that this was so. Some political scientists maintained that if nation A took over the computerocracy of nation B, and nation B did the same to nation A, then international equilibrium would again be restored. What had become everyday reality could no longer be described in terms of the old, traditional politics, or even by common sense, which still distinguished between natural phenomena, like a hailstorm, and man-made ones, like a bombing attack.

Elections were still held for political parties, but each party boasted of having not the best economic program but the best computer, one that would solve all social ills and problems. Whenever two computers disagreed, the government ostensibly decided; but in reality the arbiter was another computer. It will be better to give a concrete example.

For several decades the three major branches of the United States armed forces, the army, navy, and air force, had been struggling among themselves for supremacy. Each tried to get the largest share of the military allocation in the budget at the expense of the others. Each kept its newest weapons secret from the others. To learn these secrets was one of the main tasks of the President's advisers. Each service had its own headquarters, its own security system, its own codes, and—obviously!—its own computer. Each kept cooperation with the others to the absolute minimum, just enough so the government wouldn't fall apart. Indeed, the main concern of each successive administration was to see that a minimum of unity was maintained in the government of the country and the conduct of foreign policy.

Even in the previous century no one knew what the real military strength of the United States was, because that strength was presented to the people differently, depending on whether a White House spokesman was speaking or an opposing presidential candidate. But nowadays the devil himself could not make head or tail of the situation.

Meanwhile, in addition to computer rule, which was gradually replacing natural, human rule, there appeared certain phenomena that once would have been called natural; but now no one knew by what or by whom they were caused, if indeed they were caused by anything or anyone at all. Acid rain had been known in the twentieth century. But now there were rains so corrosive that they destroyed roads, power lines, and factory roofs, and it was impossible to determine whether they were caused by pollution or by enemy sabotage. It was that way with everything. Livestock were stricken, but was the disease natural or artificial? The hurricane that ravaged the coast—was it a chance thing, or was it engineered by an invisible swarm of micrometeorological agents, each as small as a virus, covertly diverting ocean air masses? Was the drought natural—however murderous—or was it, too, caused by a skillful diversion of the rain clouds?

These calamities beset not just the United States but the entire world. Again, some saw in this evidence of their natural origin; others, again, were convinced that the reason they were pandemic was that all countries now had at their disposal unhuman means of striking at any distance and were inflicting damage on one another, while declaring officially that they were doing nothing of the sort. Caught in the act, a saboteur could not be cross-examined: synsects and artificial microbes were mute. Meteorological counterintelligence, seismic espionage, reconnaissance teams of epidemiologists, geneticists, and even hydrographers had their hands full. An ever larger share of world science was enlisted in this military intelligence work. Hurricanes, crop failures, rising mortality rates in cattle, and even meteor showers were suspected of being intentional. (Note, by the way, that the idea of guiding asteroids to fall on enemy territory, causing terrible devastation, had arisen in the twentieth century and was considered *interesting*.)

New disciplines were taught in the military academies: crypto-offensive and crypto-defensive strategies, the cryptology of counter-counterintelligence (the covert enticement-deception of agents raised to the next power), applied enigmatics, and finally "cryptocryptics," which presented in a secret manner the secret use of weapons so secret that there was no way *anyone* could tell them from innocent phenomena of nature.

Blurred, also, was the distinction between real and spurious hostilities. In order to turn its people against another nation, a country would produce on its *own* territory "natural" catastrophes so obviously artificial that its citizens were bound to believe the charge that the enemy was responsible. When it came out that a certain large and wealthy nation, in offering aid to those that were underdeveloped and overpopulated, supplemented the provisions it sold (cheaply) of sago, wheat, corn, and potato flour with a drug that diminished sexual potency, the Third World became enraged. This was now an undercover, antinatural war.

Thus peace was war, and war peace. Although the catastrophic consequences of this trend for the future were clear— a mutual victory indistinguishable from universal destruction— the world continued to move in that fatal direction. It was not a totalitarian conspiracy, as Orwell once imagined, that made peace war, but the technological advances that effaced the boundary between the natural and the artificial in every area of human life, even in extraterrestrial space.

When there is no longer any difference between natural and artificial protein, or between natural and artificial intelligence—say the theoreticians of knowledge, the philosophers—

then neither can one distinguish a misfortune that is intentional from one for which no one is to blame.

As light, pulled irresistibly into the heart of a stellar black hole, cannot escape that gravitational trap, so humanity, pulled by the forces of mutual antagonism into the heart of matter's secrets, fell into the trap of technology, a trap of its own making. The decision to invest everything in new weapons was not made by governments, statesmen, generals, corporate interests, or pressure groups, but by the ever-growing fear that *someone else* would be first to hit upon the discoveries and technologies affording the *ultimate advantage.* This paralyzed traditional politics. The negotiators at summit meetings could not negotiate, because their willingness to relinquish a new weapon would only indicate, in the eyes of the other side, that they had another, newer weapon up their sleeve. . . .

By now the impossibility of disarmament had been proved mathematically. I have seen the mathematical model of the so-called general theory of conflicts; it shows why arms talks cannot produce results. At summit meetings certain decisions are reached. But when it takes longer to reach a decision promoting peace than it does to develop the kind of military innovations that radically change the very situation under negotiation, then any decision, at the moment of its acceptance, is an anachronism.

It is as if the ancients had debated so long about banning their "Greek fire" that by the time they agreed to ban it, Berthold Schwarz had appeared with his gunpowder. When one decides "today" about something that existed "yesterday," the decision moves from the present into the past and thereby becomes an empty game.

It was this that finally, at the end of the twenty-first century, forced the world powers into a new type of agreement, an agreement that opened up a new era in the history of the human race. But that is a subject that belongs to the twenty-second century and therefore lies outside the scope of these remarks.

Later, if I am able, I will devote a separate discussion to it—describing the next chapter of general history, a remarkable chapter, in which Earth, emerging from the era of antagonisms, truly frees itself from one technological trap, but steps into another, as if her destiny is to go forever from the frying pan into the fire.

# THE WORLD AS
# CATACLYSM

## Introduction

Books with titles like this one began to appear at the end of the twentieth century, but the image of the world contained in them did not become generally known until the next century, for only then did the discoveries germinating in widely separated branches of knowledge come together into a new synthesis. That synthesis—to put it bluntly—marked an anti-Copernican revolution in astronomy, in which our notion of the place we occupy in the Universe was stood on its head.

Pre-Copernican astronomy put the Earth in the center of the world; Copernicus deposed it from its privileged position when he discovered that ours is but one of many planets orbiting the Sun. Over the centuries, advances in astronomy strengthened the Copernican hypothesis, showing that not only was Earth not the central body in the solar system but that the system itself was located on the periphery of our Galaxy, the Milky Way. We lived "nowhere in particular" in the Universe, in a stellar suburb.

Astronomy studied the evolution of the stars, biology the

evolution of life on Earth; and the paths of their investigations met—or, rather, converged like two tributaries of a river. Astronomy took for its province the question of the incidence of life in the Universe, and theoretical biology lent its assistance to the task. Thus, in the middle of the twentieth century, CETI (Communication with Extraterrestrial Intelligence) came into being, the first program dedicated to the search for other civilizations.

But the search, conducted for several decades, utilizing ever better and more powerful instruments, found no alien civilization or any trace of a radio signal. So arose the enigma of the silentium universi. The "cosmic silence" received some publicity in the seventies, when it was taken up by the media. The undetectability of "other intelligences" was incomprehensible to scientists. The biologists had already determined what physical-chemical conditions facilitated the emergence of life from inert matter—and the conditions were not at all exceptional. The astronomers proved the existence of numerous planets around various stars. Observations indicated that a high percentage of the stars in our Galaxy had planets. The obvious conclusion was that life arose frequently in the course of ordinary cosmic changes, that its evolution should be a natural phenomenon in the Universe, and that the crowning of the evolutionary tree with the emergence of intelligent beings likewise belonged to the normal order of things. But, over the decades, the repeated failure to receive extraterrestrial signals, despite the increasing number of observatories that joined the search, contradicted this image of a populated cosmos.

According to the science of the astronomers, biochemists, and biologists, the Universe was full of stars like the Sun and planets like the Earth; by the law of large numbers, therefore, life should be developing on innumerable globes, but radio monitoring indicated, everywhere, a dead void.

The scientists who belonged to CETI and then SETI (Search for Extraterrestrial Intelligence) created various *ad hoc* hypotheses to reconcile the universal presence of life with its universal silence. At first they said that the average distance between civilizations equaled fifty to a hundred light-years. Later they had to increase the distance to six hundred and then to a thousand light-years. And there were hypotheses about the self-destructiveness of intelligence—such as von Hörner's, which connected the psychozoic "density" of the Universe with its barrenness, claiming that suicide threatened every civilization, as nuclear war was now threatening humanity. The organic evolution of life took billions of years, but its final, technological phase lasted barely a few dozen centuries. Other hypotheses pointed to the dangers that the twentieth century encountered even in the peaceful expansion of technology, whose side effects devastated the reproductive capacities of the biosphere.

Someone said, paraphrasing the famous words of Wittgenstein, "Whereof one cannot speak, thereof one must make poetry." Perhaps Olaf Stapledon, in his fantasy *Last and First Men,* was the first to express our destiny, in this sentence: "The stars create man, and the stars kill him." At the time, however, in the 1930s, these words contained more poetry than truth; they were a metaphor, not a hypothesis qualifying for citizenship in the realm of science.

But any text can hold more meaning than its author gave it. Four hundred years ago, Francis Bacon contended that flying machines were possible, as well as machines that would speed across the Earth and travel on the sea bottom. He certainly did not conceive such devices in any concrete way; but we, reading his words today, not only know that they have come true but also expand their meaning with a multitude of details familiar to us, which only adds weight to his statements.

Something similar happened with the idea that I expressed at the American-Soviet conference of CETI in Burakan in the year 1971. (My text can be found in the book *Problems of CETI,* published by Mir in Moscow in 1975.) I wrote then:

If the distribution of civilizations in the universe is *not* a matter of chance but is determined by astrophysical conditions of which we are ignorant, though they may be observable phenomena, then there will be less chance of contact the stronger the connection is between the location of the civilization and the nature of its stellar environment—that is, the more unlike a random distribution is the distribution of civilizations in space. One cannot, *a priori,* rule out the possibility that there exist astronomically observable indicators of the presence of civilization. . . . Consequently, the CETI program should also make allowance for the *passing* nature of our astrophysical knowledge, since new discoveries will influence and alter CETI's most fundamental assumptions.

And that is exactly what happened—or, rather, what is slowly happening. As from the scattered pieces of a jigsaw puzzle, a new picture is emerging from new discoveries in galactic astronomy, from new models for the genesis of the planets and the stars, from the composition of radioisotopes recently found in meteors of the solar system. The history of the solar system is being reconstructed, and the origin of life on Earth, with an import as exciting as it is contrary to all we have accepted until now.

To put the matter most concisely: the hypotheses that reconstruct the past ten billion years of the Milky Way's existence tell us that man emerged because the Universe is a place of catastrophe; that Earth, together with life, owes its existence to a peculiar sequence of catastrophes. It was as a result of violent cataclysms that the Sun gave birth to its family of planets. The solar system emerged from a series of catastrophic disturbances, and only after that could life arise, develop, and eventually establish dominion over the Earth. In the next billion-year period, during which man

THE WORLD AS CATACLYSM

had no chance to emerge because there was no room on the evolutionary tree, another catastrophe opened the way for anthropogenesis by killing hundreds of millions of Earth's creatures.

Creation through destruction (and consequent release of tensions) occupies the central place in this new picture of the world. Or one could put it thus: Earth arose because the proto-Sun entered a region of destruction; life arose because Earth left that region; man arose because in the next billion years destruction once again descended on Earth.

Stubbornly opposing the indeterminism of quantum mechanics, Einstein said, "God does not play dice with the world." By this he meant that chance cannot decide atomic phenomena. It turned out, however, that God plays dice not only on the atomic scale but with the galaxies, the stars, the planets, the birth of life, and the emergence of intelligence. We owe our existence as much to catastrophes that occurred at the right place and the right time as to those that did *not* take place in other epochs and places. We came into the world having passed—during the history of our star, then of the planet, then of biogenesis and evolution—through the eyes of many needles. The nine billion years separating the protosolar cloud of gases from *Homo sapiens* can therefore be compared to a gigantic slalom in which no gate was missed. We know now that there were many such "gates," and that any veering from the slalom run would have precluded the rise of man. What we do not know is how "wide" was this track, with its curves and gates—or, in other words, the probability of this "perfect run" whose goal was anthropogenesis.

So the world that the science of the next century will recognize will be a group of *random* catastrophes, creative as well as destructive. Note that the *group* is random, whereas each of the catastrophes in it conforms to the laws of physics.

# I

In roulette, losses are the rule for the vast majority of players. Otherwise, every Monte Carlo–type gambling casino would quickly go bankrupt. The player who leaves the gaming table with a profit is the exception to the rule. The one who wins often is a rare exception, and the one who makes a fortune because the ball lands on his number almost every time is an extraordinary exception; his incredible luck is written up in the papers.

A player can take no credit for a run of wins, because there is no betting strategy that will guarantee a win. The roulette wheel is an instrument of chance; that is, its end states cannot be predicted. Since the ball always stops at one of thirty-six numbers, the player has one chance out of thirty-six to win in every game. The player who places his bet on the same number twice has one chance in 1,296 to win twice, because the probabilities of chance events not interdependent (as on the roulette wheel) must be multiplied by one another. The probability of winning three in a row is 1:46,656. The chance is very small, but it is calculable, because the number of end states of every game is the same: thirty-six. If, however, in calculating the player's chances, we wished to take into account incidental phenomena (earthquakes, bomb attacks, the player's death from a heart attack, etc.), the task would become impossible. Similarly, when someone picks flowers in a meadow under artillery fire and returns home safe, bouquet in hand, his survival cannot be put into statistical form, either. It cannot be done, although the incalculability—and, therefore, the unpredictability—has nothing to do with the kind of unpredictability that characterizes quantum-atomic phenomena. The fate of the flower picker under fire could be made a statistic only if there were very many flower pickers, and if, in addition, the distribution of the flowers in the meadow were known, and the time of their picking, and the average number of shells per unit of shelled surface.

The determination of this statistic is complicated, moreover, by the fact that the shells that miss the picker destroy flowers, thereby changing their distribution in the meadow. The picker who is killed is dropped from the game of picking flowers under fire, just as the roulette player who was lucky at the start but then lost his shirt is dropped.

An observer watching the group of galaxies for billions of years could treat them like roulette wheels or meadows with flower pickers and discover the statistical laws to which the stars and planets are subject. From that, he would be able to establish how often life appears in the Universe and how often it evolves to the point where intelligent beings arise.

Such an observer could have been a long-lived civilization —or, more precisely, successive generations of its astronomers.

If, however, the meadow with flowers is shelled in a chaotic fashion (which means that the density of shots does not fluctuate around a certain average and therefore is not calculable), or if the roulette wheel is not "honest," then even such an observer will not be able to determine the statistics of the frequency of intelligence in the Universe.

The impossibility of determining such a statistic is practical rather than theoretical. It does not lie in the nature of matter itself, like the Heisenberg uncertainty principle, but "only" in the incalculable overlapping of different random series, which are independent of one another and take place on varied scales of magnitude: galactic, stellar, planetary, and molecular.

A galaxy treated as a roulette wheel on which life can be "won" is not an "honest" roulette wheel. An honest roulette wheel manifests one and only one probability distribution (1:36 for each play). For roulette wheels that are shaken, that change shape during the game, that keep using different balls, there is no such statistical uniformity. All roulette wheels and all spiral galaxies are certainly similar to one another, but they are not exactly the same. A galaxy can behave like a roulette wheel placed near a stove; when the stove is hot, the heat will distort the disk, which will, in turn, affect the distribution of the winning numbers. A brilliant physicist can measure the influence of temperature on the roulette wheel, but if, in addition, the floor shakes from the trucks outside, his measurement will be off.

In this sense, the galactic game of life and death is a game played on a loaded roulette wheel.

Earlier, I referred to Einstein's belief that God does not play dice with the world. I can now expand on what I said there. God not only plays dice with the world, he also plays an honest game—with perfect, identical dice—but only on the smallest scale, the atomic. Galaxies, on the other hand, are huge divine roulette wheels that are not honest. Please note that "honesty" here is understood mathematically (statistically) and not morally.

Observing a radioactive element, we can establish its half life—that is, how long one has to wait for half its atoms to decay. This decay is governed by statistically honest chance, since it is the same throughout the Universe for this element. Whether it sits in the laboratory, in the depths of the Earth, in a meteor, or in a cosmic nebula, its atoms behave the same way.

Whereas a galaxy, a mechanism that produces stars, planets, and occasionally life, does so—as a mechanism of chance—dishonestly, because incalculably.

Its creations are governed neither by determinism nor by the sort of indeterminism we find in the world of quanta. Therefore the course of the galactic "game for life" can be known only *ex post facto*, after we have won. One can reconstruct what has taken place—although it was not, in the beginning, foreseeable—but not with exactitude; it is like re-creating the history of human tribes in the era when people were still illiterate and left behind no chronicles or documents, only the work of their hands, which the archaeologist unearths. Galactic cosmology then becomes "stellar-planetary archaeology." This archaeology studies the particular game whose winning stake is *us*.

## II

A good three-quarters of the galaxies, like our Milky Way, are spiral disks with a nucleus and two arms. This galactic formation of gaseous clouds, dust, and stars (which gradually are born and die in it) revolves, its nucleus whirling at a greater angular velocity than the arms, which, falling behind, bend, thereby giving the whole the shape of a spiral.

The arms, however, do not move at the same speed as the stars.

A spiral galaxy owes its unchanging form to its *density waves*, in which the stars behave like molecules in an ordinary gas.

Orbiting at different speeds, the stars that are considerably removed from the nucleus remain outside the arm, while those near the nucleus overtake and pass through the spiral arm. Only the stars halfway out from the nucleus move at the same velocity as the arms. This is the so-called synchronous (corotational) circle. About five billion years ago, the cloud of gases from which the Sun and the planets were to form was situated near the inner edge of a spiral arm. It overtook that arm slowly—on the order of one kilometer per second. The cloud, entering deep into the density wave, became contaminated by isotopes of iodine and plutonium, the radioactive residue of a supernova that had exploded in the vicinity. The isotopes decayed, until another element, xenon, was formed from them. Meanwhile, the cloud was compressed by the density wave in which it moved, and this caused condensation until a young star—the Sun—arose. At the end of this period, some four and a half billion years ago, another supernova exploded in the neighborhood; it contaminated the circumsolar nebula (not all the protosolar gas had been concentrated yet in the Sun) with radioactive aluminum. This hastened, perhaps even caused, the emergence of the planets. Computer simulations show that, in order for a disk of gases whirling around a young star to undergo segmentation and condense into planets, some outside intervention is necessary, like the giant push supplied by the supernova that exploded not far from the Sun.

How do we know all this? From the composition of radioisotopes in the meteors of the solar system. Knowing the half life of the isotopes of iodine, plutonium, and aluminum, we can calculate when the protosolar cloud was contaminated by them. This took place at least twice; a different time of decay enables us to establish that the first contamination took place shortly after the protosolar cloud entered the inner edge of the galactic arm, and the second contamination (by radioactive aluminum) occurred some three hundred million years later.

The Sun, therefore, spent the earliest phase of its development in a region of strong radiation and shock waves that caused the formation of the planets; then, accompanied by the already cooling and solidifying planets, it left that zone. It came out into a region of high vacuum free of stellar catastrophes; thus life was able to develop on Earth without lethal disturbances.

This picture puts a big question mark over the Copernican idea that says the Earth (together with the Sun) does *not* occupy a special, favored place, but a "typical" one.

Had the Sun been on the far periphery of the Galaxy and, traveling slowly, *not* crossed a spiral arm, it certainly would not have formed the planets. Planet formation requires "midwife assistance" in the form of violent events, such as a shock wave from an exploding supernova (at least one).

Had the Sun, in giving birth to the planets, been close to the galactic nucleus, thus traveling faster than the arms of the spiral, it would have passed through them often. Frequent irradiations and shocks would then have made the emergence of life on Earth impossible, or would have destroyed it in an early phase of development.

Similarly, had the Sun orbited at the exact corotational point of the Galaxy, never leaving its arm, life would also not have been able to establish itself on our planet. Sooner or later it would have been killed by a neighboring supernova (supernovas explode most often within the galactic arms). Also, the average distance between stars is considerably smaller within the arms than between the arms.

Therefore, the conditions favoring planet formation prevail *within* the spiral arms, while the conditions that contribute to the emergence and development of life prevail in the space *between* the arms.

These conditions are not met by the stars circling near the nucleus of the Galaxy, or by the stars on its rim, or, finally, by the stars whose orbits coincide with the corotational circle—only by those in the vicinity of this circle.

One also has to realize that an eruption of a supernova too close by, instead of "squeezing" the protosolar cloud and accelerating its planetary condensation, would scatter it like dandelion fluff. Too distant an explosion, on the other hand, might be an insufficient spur to planet formation. So the successive explosions of the supernovas in the neighborhood of the Sun must have been "properly" synchronized with the successive stages of its development as a star, as a planetary system, and, finally, as a system in which life arose.

The protosolar cloud was a "player" who approached the roulette wheel with the necessary initial capital, who increased that capital by playing and winning, and who then left the casino in time, preserving everything his run of luck had given him.

It appears that biogenic planets, and therefore planets capable of giving rise to civilizations, should be found primarily near the corotational circle of the Galaxy.

If we accept this reconstruction of the history of our system, we will be forced to revise our previous notions regarding the psychozoic density of the Universe.

We are fairly sure that none of the stars in the Sun's vicinity—within a radius of fifty light-years—is home to any civilization that possesses a communications technology at least equal to ours.

The radius of the corotational circle is about $10^5$ parsecs—that is, 34,000 light-years. The whole Galaxy has more than 150 billion stars. Assuming that a third of the stars are located in the nucleus and the thick bases of the spiral arms, we obtain—for the arms themselves—a total of 100 billion stars. We do not know how thick to make the torus, a figure in the shape of an automobile tire, which, if drawn around the corotational circle, will contain the whole zone favoring the emergence of life-bearing planets. Let us assume that in the zone that makes up the biogenic torus lie a hundred-thousandth of all the stars of the galactic spiral—that means millions. The entire circumference of the corotational circle is about 215,000 light-years. If *each* of the stars there produced one civilization, the average distance between two inhabited planets would equal 5 light-years. But the stars near the corotational circle are not spread out evenly in space. Moreover, planet-bearing stars are more likely to be found *within* the spiral arms, and stars with a planet on which life can evolve without fatal disturbances are more likely to be found in the space *between* the arms, where there is less exposure to stellar upheavals. However, most of the stars are inside the arms, where stars are most densely concentrated.

Therefore one should seek signals of extraterrestrial intelligence along the corotational arc *ahead* of the Sun and *behind* the Sun on the galactic plane—that is, between the stellar clouds of Perseus and Sagittarius, because the stars there, like our Sun, have the galactic passage behind them and are now moving, like our solar system, in the empty space between the arms.

But these simplified statistical reflections have little value. Let us return to our reconstructed history of the Sun and its planets.

Where the corotational circle intersects the spiral arms, their thickness is about three hundred parsecs. The protosolar gas cloud, moving along an orbit at an angle of seven or eight degrees to the plane of the Galaxy, entered the arm for the first time about 4.9 billion years ago. For three hundred million years the cloud underwent the stormy conditions of passage through the entire width of the arm; since it left the arm, it has been traveling through calm space. That trip has lasted much longer than the passage through the arm, because the corotational circle, along which the Sun moves, intersects the spiral arms at a sharp angle, making the arc of the solar orbit between the arms longer than the arc within the arm.

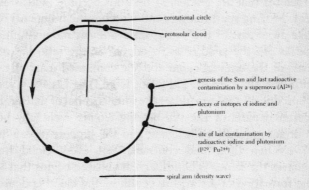

The diagram (after L. S. Marochkin, *Priroda* [Nature], no. 6, 1982) shows our Galaxy, the radius of the corotational circle, and the orbit of the solar system around the galactic nucleus. The speed with which the Sun and the planets move relative to the spiral arms is a subject of controversy. The diagram shows our system having passed through *both* arms. If that was the case, then the first passage was made by a cloud of gas and dust, which began condensing noticeably only when it crossed the second galactic arm. Whether we have behind us one or two passages is not important, because it has to do with the age of the cloud—that is, with when it first formed—and not with when it began the fragmentation that was the first stage of astrogenesis. Stars are born in a similar way even now.

An isolated cloud cannot contract gravitationally into a star because it would preserve its angular momentum (in accordance with the laws of motion) and rotate faster the smaller its radius. If eventually a star formed, it would rotate at the equator with a speed exceeding light, but this is impossible: the centrifugal forces would tear it apart much earlier. So stars emerge in great numbers from separate fragments of a cloud, in the course of processes that are gradual at first but become increasingly violent. Moving apart during condensation, the fragments of cloud take away part of the young stars' angular momentum. If one speaks of "the yield of astrogenesis" as the ratio between the mass of the original cloud and the combined mass of the stars formed from it, that yield is not large. The Galaxy is therefore a "producer" that squanders the initial capital of matter. But the scattered parts of the star-bearing clouds eventually begin to contract gravitationally again, and the process repeats itself.

When the cloud contracts, not every cloud fragment behaves the same. When the great collapse begins that leads to the formation of a star, the center of the cloud is denser than its periphery. For this reason, the star-creating fragments vary in size. In the center, they are two to four times the Sun's size; on the circumference, ten to twenty times. From inner condensates there can form small, long-lived stars that burn with more or less the same brightness for billions of years. The Sun is one of these. On the other hand, the large, peripheral stars can generate supernovas, which, after an astronomically short life, are blown apart by powerful explosions.

How our particular cloud began to condense we do not know; all we can re-create is the fate of that local fragment in which the Sun and the planets had their origin. When the process began, the nearby supernovas contaminated the protosolar cloud with radioactive particles. At least two such contaminations occurred. The first time, the protosolar cloud was contaminated with isotopes of iodine and plutonium, probably near the inner edge of the spiral arm; the second time (three hundred million years later), deep inside the spiral, another supernova bombarded it with the radioactive isotope of aluminum.

From the degree to which these isotopes have been transformed, by radioactive decay, into other elements, one can tell when each contamination occurred. The short-lived isotopes of iodine and plutonium went to a stable isotope of xenon, and the radioactive isotope of aluminum became magnesium. The xenon and the magnesium have been found in meteors of our solar system. Comparing these data with the age of the Earth's crust (using as a yardstick the times of decay of uranium and thorium, the long-lived isotopes contained in it), one can reconstruct approximate if not exact "scenarios" of the solar cosmogony.

The diagram shows the scenario by which a gaseous cloud first passed through the spiral nine and a half billion years ago. Its density was still subcritical then, so there was no fragmentation and formation of condensates. That occurred only after its entrance into the next arm of the Galaxy, 4.6 billion years ago. On the outer edge of the condensates, conditions favored the rise of supernovas; on the inside, of smaller stars, like the Sun. Subjected to compression and the explosions of the supernovas, the protosolar fragment changed into the young Sun and the planets, comets, and meteors. This cosmogonic scenario is simplified: the fragmentation of the gaseous clouds is random; through the enormous expanse of the arms run shock fronts, produced by various cataclysms; erupting supernovas can take part in generating such fronts.

Galaxies continue to give birth to stars, because the Universe in which we live, while certainly not young, is not yet old. Computer simulations reaching far into the future show that in the end all the star-generating material will be depleted, the stars will be extinguished, and whole galaxies will "vaporize" into radiation and particles.

From this "thermodynamic death" we are separated by some $10^{100}$ years. Long before that—in $10^{15}$ years—all the stars will lose their planets from having other stars pass close to them. The planets, whether lifeless or inhabited, torn from their orbits by strong perturbations, will be swallowed in endless darkness and a temperature close to absolute zero. Paradoxically, it is easier to describe what will become of the Universe in $10^{15}$ or in $10^{100}$ years, or what took place in the first few minutes of its existence, than to reconstruct the different stages of solar and terrestrial history. It is even more difficult to foresee what will become of our system when it leaves the calm space that stretches between Perseus and Sagittarius, between the stellar clouds of the two galactic arms. Assuming that the difference between the speed of the Sun and the spiral equals one kilometer per second, we shall reach the next spiral in five hundred million years.

In dealing with cosmogony, astrophysics proceeds like a detective gathering circumstantial evidence: there are only a few "footprints and exhibits," from which, like the scattered pieces of a jigsaw puzzle (and many of the pieces are lost), one must put together a consistent whole. What is worse, it appears that from these bits of evidence one can build a number of unidentical models. Not all the data, especially in the case that interests us, are numerically determinable (for example, the difference between the orbital speed of the Sun and that of the galactic spiral). In addition, the spiral arms themselves are not so compact, and do not move through space so clearly and regularly, as in our diagram. Finally, all spiral nebulae are similar, but similar in the way people are who are of different heights, weights, ages, races, sexes, and so on.

Nevertheless, cosmological work on the Milky Way is getting closer and closer to the true state of things. Stars are born mainly inside the spiral arms; supernovas explode most frequently inside those arms; the Sun is definitely located near the corotational circle, therefore not just "anywhere" in the Galaxy —because, as was shown, the conditions prevailing in the corotational zone are different both from those near the nucleus and from those on the edges of the spiral disk.

With computer simulation cosmologists will be able, in a short time, to consider a multitude of variations of star and planetary formation, which not long ago was extremely tedious and time-consuming work. Meanwhile, observational astrophysics is providing new and more precise data for these simulations. The investigation, however, is still in progress; the material evidence and the mathematical guesswork, pointing to the Perpetrators, have acquired the force of a solidly based hypothesis. These are not groundless speculations. The indictment of the spiral nebula for being both mother and infanticide has been placed before the tribunal of astronomy. The trial goes on; the final verdict has not yet been reached.

## III

In a discussion of the history of our solar system in the Galaxy, it is suitable to use legal terminology: cosmology, engaged in the reconstruction of past events, acts like an examining magistrate in a case where there is no hard evidence against the accused, only a set of incriminating circumstances. The cosmologist, like the judge, tries to determine what happened in a given concrete instance. He does not have to worry about how often such an instance may occur or what the probability of its occurring was.

But in contrast to the judiciary, cosmology tries to learn much more about the matter. If a champagne bottle—with thick glass and the characteristic hollow at the bottom—is thrown out the window and breaks, then by repeating the experiment we will see that the neck and the bottom usually end up in single pieces while the rest of the glass breaks into many fragments of different shapes.

There is no precise answer to the question of how often, in breaking bottles, one can obtain exactly the same fragments. One can establish only how many pieces the bottles break into most often. Such a statistic is easily arrived at by repeating the experiment many times under the same conditions (the distance the bottle falls, whether it falls on concrete or wood, etc.). But it may also happen that the bottle, in falling, will hit a football kicked by one of the children playing in the yard, will thus bounce and fly through the window of the elderly lady on the floor below who keeps goldfish in an aquarium, will fall into the aquarium, sink, and fill with water, unbroken. Everyone will agree that, although highly improbable, such an event is still possible; people will see it not as a supernatural phenomenon, a miracle, but only as an extraordinary coincidence.

Yet such coincidences cannot be put into statistics. Besides Newton's laws of motion and the glass's strength, one would have to take into consideration how often the children played football in the yard, how often the football collided with falling bottles during the game, how often the old lady left her window open, how often the fish tank stood near the window; if we wanted to have a "general theory of champagne bottles that fall into aquariums undamaged after being hit by footballs," taking into account all the bottles, children, houses, yards, goldfish, aquariums, and windows in the world, we would never accomplish it with statistics.

The key question in re-creating the history of the solar system and life on Earth is: Did something happen on the order of simple bottle-breaking, which could be put into statistics, or was it, instead, something like the football and the aquarium?

Phenomena that are statistically calculable do not become statistically incalculable suddenly, at a well-defined boundary, but, rather, by degrees. The scholar takes a position of cognitive optimism; that is, he assumes that the subjects he studies will yield to calculation. It is nicest if they do so deterministically: the angle of incidence is equal to the angle of reflection; a body immersed in water loses exactly as much of its weight as the weight of the water it displaces; and so on. It is not quite so nice if calculable probability has to substitute for certainty. But it is not nice at all when absolutely nothing can be calculated. It is commonly said that when nothing can be calculated and nothing predicted, one has chaos. Yet "chaos" in the exact sciences does not mean that we know nothing whatever, that what we have to deal with is absolute disorder. There is no "absolute disorder." Even in the tale of the bottle and the football there is no chaos. Every event, taken separately, obeys the laws of physics, and of deterministic physics, not quantum physics, because we can measure the force with which the child kicked the ball, the angle of impact between bottle and ball, the speed of both bodies at that instant, the path the bottle described when it bounced off the ball, and the speed with which it fell into the aquarium and filled with water. Each step of the sequence, taken separately, is subject to mechanics and statistics, but the *sequence itself* is not (that is, one cannot establish how often a thing that has happened will happen).

The point is that all theories of "broad scope" in physics are incomplete, because they say nothing about the initial states. The initial states have to be brought into the theory from the outside. It is obvious, however, that when some initial state must be achieved precisely by chance in order to produce the initial state of the next occurrence, also precisely defined, and so on, then a certainty that transcends the realm of probabilities becomes an unknown, about which nothing can be said except that "something very unusual took place."

That is why I said at the beginning that the world is a group of random catastrophes governed by precise laws.

To the question "How often does what happened with the Sun and the Earth happen in the Universe?" there is no answer yet, because we are not sure in which category of events to place the case.

With advances in astrophysics and cosmology the matter will gradually be clarified. Much that the experts said at the CETI meeting in Burakan in 1971 is now out of date or has been shown to be incorrect. In ten or twenty years, no doubt, many things that are mysterious today will be explained.

The Moon played a large if not decisive role in the emergence of life on Earth. Life could start only in aqueous solutions of certain chemical compounds, and not in the deep seas but in coastal shallows. The frequent but gentle mixing produced by the tidal ebb and flow caused by the Moon hastened the protobiogenesis in these solutions.

But less is known about how the moons of the planets came into being than about how the planets themselves formed. For now, one cannot rule out the possibility that the formation of planetary satellites is as "extraordinary" as the story of the bottle and the aquarium. An ordinary shock wave from a supernova seems sufficient to cause ring fragmentation of a protosolar nebular disk, but for moons to condense around planets, something like the intersection of two circular waves may be needed, as when two stones are dropped into water (not far apart) and the ripples radiate outward. In other words, for moons to form, a second supernova may be needed, also not far from the protosolar system.

If not all these questions are answered, there will still be some answers, and thus the probability of life's arising in the Universe—the biogenetic yield or frequency—will acquire an approximate numerical value. The value may prove to be large, in which case we will be right to expect the presence of life in an innumerable wealth of forms on the multitude of planets in the trillion galaxies that surround us.

But even if that happens, books with the titles I predicted will appear. I will now proceed to show the reason. The grim truth is: without a global destruction of life, man would not have arisen.

## IV

How does the new view of life in the Universe differ from the old? We have long known that the birth of life on a planet must be preceded by a long chain of specific events, beginning with the formation of a long-lived and evenly burning star like the Sun, and that this star must create a planetary family. But we did not know that the arms of a spiral galaxy are (or can be) alternate cradles and guillotines of life, depending on the stage of development of the star-generating material when it passes through the spiral and on the place in the arm where the passage occurs.

At the symposium in Burakan I was the only one to hold that the distribution of life-generating heavenly bodies was dependent on events of extraplanetary and extrastellar (galactic) magnitude. Obviously, I, too, was unaware that the chain of events included the motion of the star-generating cloud around the corotational circle; that inside the cloud, the "right" synchronization of astrogenesis and eruptions of supernovas on the cloud's circumference was necessary; and moreover— *conditio sine qua non est longa vita*—that the system where biogenesis began had to depart immediately from the spiral's

89

stormy zone for the calm expanse of space between the arms.

At the end of the seventies it became fashionable to include in cosmological hypotheses a factor called the Anthropic Principle. This factor reduces the enigma of the initial state of the Universe to an argument *ad hominem:* if conditions had been very different, the question would not have arisen, since there would have been no one to ask it.

It is not hard to see that as a cosmological criterion the Anthropic Principle (the appearance of *Homo sapiens* was inherent in the Big Bang) has about as much cognitive value as the "Schnapps Principle."

True, the production of schnapps was made possible thanks to the properties of matter in *this* Universe, but one can perfectly well imagine the history of *this* Universe, *this* Sun, *this* Earth, and *this* human race *without* the emergence of schnapps. Schnapps originated because people engaged in the production of different beverages, including those that contained alcohol, sugar, juniper berries, and herbal extracts. This answer is sensible, though general. Whereas to answer the question "How did schnapps come about?" with "It came about because *such* was the initial state of the Universe" is ridiculous. One might just as well say that Volkswagens or postage stamps owe their existence to the initial state of the Universe. Such an answer explains *ignotum per ignotius.* It is also a *circulus in explicando:* that which *could* arise, did arise. But such an answer ignores the most distinctive property of the proto-Universe. According to the obligatory Big Bang Theory, the Universe was born in an explosion that simultaneously created matter, time, and space.

Traces of this world-creating explosion remain in the Universe to this day as residual radiation present everywhere in the stellar background. In the twenty billion years of the Universe's existence, the radiation of the first moment has cooled to a few degrees above absolute zero. But that residual radiation ought not to be the same across the whole canopy of sky. The Universe originated from a point of infinitely great density and in the course of $10^{-35}$ of a second expanded to the volume of a soccer ball. Even at that moment it was too large and was expanding too rapidly to remain perfectly homogeneous. Causal connections of events are limited by the maximum speed of interaction, which is the speed of light. Such connections were able to last only in regions with dimensions of $10^{-25}$ centimeter, but $10^{78}$ such regions could fit in a universe the size of a soccer ball. What took place in some regions, therefore, could not influence the events in others. And therefore the Universe ought to have expanded heterogeneously and not kept the symmetry of those everywhere-identical properties that we nevertheless observe in it. The Big Bang Theory is saved by the hypothesis that in the creational explosion an *immense number of universes* formed simultaneously. Our Universe was only one of them.

A theory published in 1982 reconciles the homogeneity of the actual Universe with the nonhomogeneity of its expansion through the premise that the proto-Universe was not a universe but a "poliverse." A poliverse hypothesis can be found in a little book of mine called *Imaginary Magnitude,* which I wrote ten years earlier, in 1972. The similarity of my speculations to the theories that appeared later gives me courage to speculate further.

Let us recall the champagne bottle that bounced off the football, flew through the open window, and fell into the aquarium. Impossible though it is to calculate the statistical probability of such an accident, we recognize that the accident was possible (that is, it did not contradict the laws of nature; it was not a miracle). And if the bottle had fallen into an aquarium full of stagnant water and dead fish and had splashed, sending a few fish eggs into a bucket of fresh water standing nearby, and if live fish were born from those eggs, it would be an event even rarer, even more exceptional than if there had been no bucket, eggs, or resultant little fish.

Suppose that the children are still playing football; that someone is still tossing champagne bottles out of the second-floor window every now and then; that the next empty bottle, bouncing off the football (which just then intersects the path of its fall), flies into the bucket, so that the little fish born from the roe are splashed out and into butter sizzling on a frying pan. The lady of the house, who had intended to make an omelet, on her return to the kitchen finds little fried fish in the pan.

Would *this* be an "absolute impossibility"? One cannot maintain that. All one can say is that it was an accident *sui generis*, one whose full course (beginning with the first champagne bottle) will never be repeated *exactly* the same way. It is just too improbable. The slightest deviation will cause the bottle not to land in the kitchen, because it will not ricochet off the football "as it should"; or it will break on the floor; or it will sink in the aquarium and nothing more will happen; or it will splash some roe but the roe will not fall into the bucket and produce fish. Then, too, the bucket could be empty, or filled with laundry soaking in a detergent lethal to fish. And so on.

When we bring the Anthropic Principle into cosmology, we are saying that the appearance of man has crowned the evolution of life on Earth with intelligence, since the emergence of intelligent beings becomes more probable the longer that evolution lasts. Leaving the terrain of what today is considered certain or reasonably certain, I will move on to what the science of the next century will contribute to the subject.

## V

First, evidence will be gathered showing that the limb of the evolutionary tree that created the mammals would not have branched and would not have given them primacy among the animals had there not been, sixty-five million years ago, between the Cretaceous and Tertiary, a catastrophe in the form of an enormous, 3.5-to-4-trillion-ton meteorite.

Up to that time, the dominant animals were the reptiles. They reigned on land, on water, and in the air for two hundred million years. Attempting to explain their abrupt extinction at the end of the Mesozoic, the evolutionists attributed to these reptiles the traits of contemporary reptiles: cold-bloodedness, primitive organs, and a hairless body covered only by scales or horned armor. And when they reconstructed the appearance and way of life of these animals on the basis of the skeletal fragments found, they did so according to their biases. One could call this "mammal chauvinism." Paleontologists have said, for example, that the large reptiles, like the brontosaurus, were incapable of moving on dry land and spent their life in shallow water, feeding on plants. Or that the two-legged reptiles, though ambulatory, were awkward, dragging long, heavy tails over the ground. And so on.

Only in the second half of the twentieth century was it learned that the Mesozoic reptiles were as warm-blooded as mammals; that many species—especially the flying ones—had a furlike coat; that the two-legged reptiles did not lumber along dragging their tails, but in speed matched the ostrich, although they weighed up to two hundred times more: the tail, held horizontally by special ligaments, served as a counterweight for the forward-leaning body when it ran. Even the largest saurians moved freely on land.

Unable to go into a comparative study of extinct and modern species here, I will give one example of the skill, never since equaled, possessed by certain flying reptiles. The "biological flying record" does not belong to the birds, and still less to the flying mammals, the bats. The largest animal of Earth's atmosphere was *Quetzalcoatlus northropi*, whose body mass exceeded man's. But it was only one of a group of species given the name Titanopterygia. These were reptiles that glided over the ocean and fed on fish. We do not know how they were able to land and take off, since the weight of their body meant that to do so they would have required a muscular strength beyond that of the animals (and birds) of today. When their fossils were found in Texas and Argentina, it was first thought that these giants of the air, equal in wingspan to a small or even medium plane (thirteen to fifteen meters), spent their lives and built their nests at the top of crags, from which they hurled themselves into the air, spreading their wings. But if they were unable to take off from level ground, they would all, to the last specimen, have been condemned to death if they landed only once in a flat place. Some of these great soarers lived off carrion—but carrion is not found on peaks. Moreover, their enormous bones were found in places devoid of mountains. For experts in aerodynamics, these reptiles present a puzzle. No explanation holds up. A colossus like Quetzalcoatlus could not light on trees; that would cause frequent injury or actual fracture to the wings. The largest specimen of flying bird known is a certain extinct vulture with a wingspan of nearly seven meters; doubling its size quadruples the force needed to rise into the air. The large flying reptiles could not take off by running, either, because their legs were too short and weak.

When the charge of "primitivism" as the cause of extinction was dropped, the opposite replaced it—overspecialization. The reptiles died out, supposedly, because they were too narrowly adapted to their environment; they perished because of a change in climate.

Climatic changes have indeed occurred in the history of the Earth. Everyone knows about the ice ages. The extinction of life at the junction of the Cretaceous and Tertiary periods was also preceded by a cooling; but the cooling did not lead to an ice age. What is more important, no change of climate ever caused the massive extinction of so many species of animals and plants at once. Their fossil remains suddenly vanish in the geological strata of the next period. The figures show that no animal survived whose body weight exceeded twenty kilograms. Never before had there been such a global annihilation. Many invertebrates became extinct then, on land and in the sea almost simultaneously. It was like a biblical plague: day turned into night, and the darkness lasted about two years. Not only could the Sun not be seen anywhere on the Earth's surface, but its rays provided less illumination than does the full moon. All the large diurnal animals died out. But the small, ratlike mammals, nocturnal scavengers, survived. Out of these remnants of the great zoocide, new species arose during the Tertiary, including the one that bore the fruit of anthropogenesis. The darkness, cutting the Earth off from the Sun's energy, destroyed most of the green vegetation, since it made photosynthesis impossible. A multitude of algae also died.

I cannot go into more detail now, but, though the mechanism and the consequences of the catastrophe were certainly more complex than is presented here, the *scope* is the same.

The balance sheet looks like this. Man could not emerge from the differentiated biological legacy of the Mesozoic, because that mass represented capital invested in species incapable of anthropogenesis. The investment (as always in evolution) was irreversible; the capital was lost. New capital began to form from the surviving vestiges of life scattered over the Earth. It increased and multiplied until the rise of the hominids and anthropoids.

If evolution's huge investment in the Thecodontia, Saurischia, Ornithischia, and in the Rhamphorhynchoidea and Pterodactyloidea had not ended in a great crash sixty-five million years ago, the mammals would not have taken over the planet. We owe our existence to that catastrophe. We emerged and multiplied into the billions only because billions of other creatures suffered annihilation. Hence the title, *The World as Cataclysm.*

The scientific search for evidence has led us only to the

random author of our species—an indirect albeit a necessary author. It was not the meteor that created us: that only opened the way. The massive destruction that laid waste the Earth thereby made room for more evolutionary experiments. It remains an open question whether, without the meteor catastrophe, intelligence would have appeared on Earth in another form —a nonhuman, nonanthropoid form.

## VI

Where there is No One—therefore no feelings, friendly or hostile, no love or hate—there are also no intentions. The Universe, being neither a Person nor the work of any Person, cannot be accused of bias in its action: it simply is what it is and does what it does. What it does is create, again and again, by destroying. Some stars "must" explode and disintegrate so that the heavy elements formed in their nuclear cauldrons can disperse and give a start—billions of years later—to planets and, once in a while, organic life. Others, supernovas, "must" undergo catastrophic destruction in order that galactic clouds of hydrogen, compressed by the explosions, can condense into sunlike, long-lived stars that calmly and steadily warm their family of planets, who also owe their existence to these catastrophes.

But must intelligence, too, begin in lethal cataclysm?

The twenty-first century will not have a definitive answer to that question. It will continue to gather evidence and will fashion a new picture of the world: a collection of random catastrophes governed by precise laws. But it will not provide the final explanation for intelligence.

It will dispel, to be sure, many illusions that persist in science. For example, it will establish beyond any doubt that a brain of high volume is not equivalent to a brain of high intelligence, for which largeness is a necessary but not a sufficient condition. The extraordinary intelligence with which dolphins are supposedly endowed because their brains are larger and more complex than man's, this dolphin intellect about which so much has been written in our time, will be shown to be a myth. A large brain was indeed needed if the dolphins were to compete successfully in the same ocean with the "stupid" sharks. It allowed them to enter and survive in a niche occupied for millions of years by predator fish—but nothing more.

From this it follows that no statement can be made regarding the chances of intelligence arising among the reptiles had there been no meteor.

A slow but practically constant growth in neural mass characterizes the evolution of *all* animals, with the exception of certain parasites. But even if that growth were to continue over a time measured in hundreds of millions of years, through the Cretaceous and Tertiary, it would not guarantee the emergence of intelligent saurians.

The crater-pocked surfaces of all the moons in our planetary system are like photographs of the past, a frozen picture of the beginning of this system, which was also created out of destruction. All the bodies orbited the young Sun in frequently intersecting paths, and collisions resulted. Thanks to these catastrophes, the large bodies—the planets—increased in mass, while the bodies of small mass, in colliding with the planets, "vanished" from the system. I said earlier that about 4.6 billion years ago the Sun and its planetary family left the stormy region of the galactic spiral and moved off into calm space. But this does not mean that the interior of the solar system was then calm. Collisions of planets with meteorites and comets were still going on when life began on Earth. Moreover, leaving the spiral arm was not like walking out of a house; radiation and stars do not suddenly cease to exist at any one point. During the first billion years of its existence, the Earth was still continually exposed to shocks, though the supernovas were distant enough not to devastate it and turn it into a dead globe. The hard radiation (X rays and gamma rays) coming from space was a factor both creative and destructive, since it accelerated the rate of mutation in the proto-organisms.

Some insects are a hundred times less vulnerable to the lethal effect of radioactivity than vertebrates. This is really very strange when you consider that the hereditary substance of all living systems is basically the same. They differ from one another in the way buildings of various cultures, epochs, and architectural styles differ; the building material—brick and stone—is the same everywhere, as is the mortar that keeps the whole together.

The difference in vulnerability to lethal radiation must have been caused by events extremely distant in time, by catastrophes in the era when the first insects (or, rather, their ancestors) came into being, about 430 million years ago. It is not impossible, however, that the "insensitivity" of certain organic forms to radiation fatal to most others developed one billion years ago.

Will the coming century witness a revival of the theory put forth by the early nineteenth-century French paleontologist and anatomist Cuvier, called catastrophism? It saw geological processes, like mountain-formation, climate changes, the rise and disappearance of seas, as violent and sudden transformations—planetary catastrophes. The theory was developed further by Cuvier's student, d'Orbigny, in the middle of the nineteenth century; according to him, the organic world of the Earth perished and arose anew many times in successive acts of creation.

This union of catastrophism with creationism was laid to rest by Darwin's theory, but the funeral was premature. Catastrophes on the largest scale, cosmic, are an indispensable condition not only for the evolution of stars but also for the evolution of life. It was the human mind that created the alternative of either "destruction or creation" and that has continued to impose it on the world since the dawn of our history. Man considered the mutual exclusiveness of destruction and creation as self-evident when he faced his own mortality and set it against his will to live. That opposition is the common foundation for all the hundreds of our cultures; one finds it in the most ancient myths, creation legends, and religious beliefs, and in the science that arose a few thousand years later. Faith as well as science endowed the visible world with properties that eliminated blind, incalculable chance as the author of all events. The war of good and evil present in all religions does not always end, in every faith, with the victory of good, but in every one it establishes a clear *order* of existence. The sacred as well as the profane rest on that universal order. Thus, chance, the ultimate arbiter of existence, was not present in any of the beliefs of the past.* Science, too, long resisted acknowledging the creative and incalculable role of chance in the shaping of reality.

Human beliefs can be divided roughly into those that offer comfort and those that offer order vis-à-vis the given world. The first type promises reward, salvation, a final reckoning of sins and merits, to be crowned in the hereafter with an ultimate justice. To an imperfect world is added a perfect continuation. Most likely such beliefs owe their great longevity, generation after generation, to their property of soothing our complaints against the world. On the other hand, the old myths, instead of offering the peace and promise of a just goodness in a well-run eternity —whatever one may say about paradise and heaven, not a scrap of chance exists there: no one will go to hell as a result of divine error or oversight, and no one will find himself in a posthumous jam because a foul-up prevents him from entering nirvana—the old myths offer an order that is often cruel but necessary. Neither the goodness nor the order resembles a lottery.

Culture exists and has always existed in order to make every accident, every kind of arbitrariness, appear in a benevolent or

*The word "chance" is not found in any scripture of any faith.

at least necessary light. The common denominator of all cultures, the source of ritual, of all commandments, of every taboo, is this: for everything there is one and only one measure. Cultures have taken chance in small, careful doses—for fun, as games and amusements. Chance, when domesticated and held in tight rein as a game or lottery, ceases to be dangerous. We play the lottery because we want to; no one forces us.

A believer can see chance in the breaking of a glass or in a wasp sting, but he does not attribute death to chance. In his thoughtless head, Divine Omnipotence and Omniscience seem to assign a *subordinate* role to accidents. And science, for as long as it could, treated chance as the effect of currently insufficient knowledge, as an ignorance that a future discovery would dispel. These are not jests; Einstein was not joking when he declared that "God does not play dice," because "He is subtle, but He is not malicious." This meant: the order of the world is difficult to know, but since it is rational, it is possible to know.

The end of the twentieth century has seen a general turning away from those thousands of years of stubbornly, desperately held beliefs. The destruction-or-creation alternative must finally be rejected. The huge clouds of dark, cold gases circling in the arms of galaxies are slowly undergoing fragmentation into parts as unpredictable as shattered glass. The laws of Nature act not *in spite of* random events but *through* them. The statistical fury of the stars, a billion times aborting in order to give birth once to life, a life slain by a chance catastrophe in millions of its species in order to yield intelligence once—this is the rule, not the exception, in the Universe.

Suns form from the destruction of other stars; the remains of protostellar clouds congeal into planets. Life is one of the rare winners in this lottery, and intelligence an even rarer winner in the subsequent draws: it owes its appearance to natural selection —that is, to death, which improves the survivors—and to catastrophes that can abruptly increase the odds for the emergence of intelligent beings.

The link between the structure of the world and the structure of life is no longer doubted, but the Universe is an enormously profligate investor, squandering its initial capital on the roulette wheels that are galaxies. (What brings regularity to the game is the law of large numbers.) Man, shaped by these properties of matter, properties that appeared when the world appeared, turns out to be a rare exception to the rule of destruction: man, the survivor of hecatombs and holocausts. Creation and destruction alternate, overlap, interact, reciprocate, and from them there is no escape or appeal.

Such is the picture that science is building little by little—so far without comment. It pieces the picture together from discoveries in biology and cosmology, like a mosaic from pebbles found one at a time. I could stop here, but I will take another moment to consider the final question that we are permitted to ask.

## VII

I have sketched a picture of the reality that the science of the twenty-first century will popularize, because even today the outlines are visible. This picture will receive the seal of approval of the best experts. The question which I wish to pursue where even speculation cannot reach has to do with the permanence of this world-view. Will it be the last?

The history of science shows that each picture of the world, in turn, was thought to be the last; then it was revised, only to crumble eventually like the pattern of a broken mosaic, and the labor of putting it together was taken up anew by the next generation. Religious beliefs stand on dogmas whose rejection has always been tantamount first to vile heresy, later to the birth of another religion. Living faith, to those who profess it, is the Ultimate Truth; there is no appeal. In science, there is nothing ultimate and everything can be appealed. The "certainties" of scientific knowledge are not all equally certain, and there is nothing to indicate that we are getting close to the Goal of Cognition, that final fusion of Immovable Knowledge with Irresistible Ignorance. Our increments of reliable knowledge, proved through concrete application, are unquestionable. In science, we know more than our nineteenth-century predecessors; they, in turn, knew more than their forefathers—but at the same time we recognize the world's inexhaustibility, the fathomlessness of its secrets, for we see that each atom, each "elementary particle," turns out to be a bottomless well. It is this astounding bottomlessness of knowledge (though everybody is accustomed now to this marathon without a finish line) that renders every "ultimate view of reality" suspect. It may be that the *principium creationis per destructionem* will prove to be but a phase of our diagnosis that applies the human measure to a thing as inhuman as the Universe. It may be that someday a *deus ex machina* will cope with these inhuman, overcomplicated measurements, inaccessible to our poor animal brains: an alienated, human-initiated machine intelligence—or, rather, the product, pretermechanical, of a human-launched evolution of synthetic mind. But here I overstep the twenty-first century into a darkness that no speculation can illumine.

# A Selected List of Science Fiction Available from Mandarin

While every effort is made to keep prices low, it is sometimes necessary to increase prices at short notice. Mandarin Paperbacks reserves the right to show new retail prices on covers which may differ from those previously advertised in the text or elsewhere.

The prices shown below were correct at the time of going to press.

| | | | |
|---|---|---|---|
| ☐ 7493 0021 3 | **Kinsman** | Ben Bova | £3.50 |
| ☐ 7493 0083 8 | **Millennium** | Ben Bova | £3.50 |
| ☐ 7493 0120 1 | **Peacekeepers** | Ben Bova | £3.50 |
| ☐ 7493 0105 8 | **The Compleat Traveller in Black** | John Brunner | £3.50 |
| ☐ 7493 0007 8 | **The Chronicles of Morgaine** | C. J. Cherryh | £4.99 |
| ☐ 7493 0154 6 | **Downbelow Station** | C. J. Cherryh | £3.99 |
| ☐ 7493 0006 X | **Exile's Gate** | C. J. Cherryh | £3.99 |
| ☐ 7493 0068 X | **Pride of Chanur** | C. J. Cherryh | £2.99 |
| ☐ 7493 0100 7 | **Serpents Reach** | C. J. Cherryh | £3.50 |
| ☐ 7493 0038 8 | **Highway of Eternity** | Clifford D. Simak | £2.99 |
| ☐ 7493 0099 X | **Off-Planet** | Clifford D. Simak | £3.50 |
| ☐ 7493 0079 5 | **Where the Evil Dwells** | Clifford D. Simak | £3.50 |
| ☐ 7493 0103 1 | **Deep Space** | Eric Frank Russell | £2.99 |
| ☐ 7493 0047 7 | **A Splendid Chaos** | John Shirley | £3.99 |
| ☐ 7493 0037 X | **Ravenmoon** | Peter Tremayne | £3.50 |

All these books are available at your bookshop or newsagent, or can be ordered direct from the publisher. Just tick the titles you want and fill in the form below.

**Mandarin Paperbacks**, Cash Sales Department, PO Box 11, Falmouth, Cornwall TR10 9EN.

Please send cheque or postal order, no currency, for purchase price quoted and allow the following for postage and packing:

UK        80p for the first book, 20p for each additional book ordered to a maximum charge of £2.00.

BFPO      80p for the first book, 20p for each additional book.

Overseas    £1.50 for the first book, £1.00 for the second and 30p for each additional book
including Eire   thereafter.

NAME (Block letters) .................................................................................................................

ADDRESS ..............................................................................................................................

......................................................................................................................................

......................................................................................................................................